Buried in the soul of one is a secret even dragons fear.

THE
FLAMES
OF
DARKNESS

BOOK ONE OF HELL'S FIRE DRAGON

LA KAYSHAL

First published in 2025 by La Kayshal
Copyright © La Kayshal 2025

If Gods exist, then so do Demons.

The arrival of one ensures the awakening

of the other.

Table of Contents

Table of Contents

PROLOGUE

25 years ago

A shadow emerged.

From the deep abyss of hell, a defiant, dark-clawed hand crept swiftly, yet it remained in the hidden depths of the crevices.

Adalward, the four-headed, golden guardian dragon sent from the Heavens to watch the Hellgate, smirked. For centuries beyond memory, nothing escaped the burning depths of hell. He had diligently ensured that and today was no different. His old bones were ready to play the game of hide and seek.

He flew closer, his four heads sniffing and eyeing the foul shadow of a doomed creature who was perhaps once a cruel human, but now a permanent inhabitant of hell.

Before the creature could rise, one of Adalward's massive, hideous jaws opened, spraying a torrent of golden flame, spilling ash across the cracked earth. The creature shrieked, and the dark claws dissolved into smoke as it plunged back into the pit, leaving the desert trembling in silence.

Hellgate was situated in a vast desert, its sands shifting like a living thing beneath the merciless sun. Each grain caught the light until the horizon burned like the edge of a forge. The wind did not whisper here. It screamed, carrying with it the scent of scorched stone and something older, something that did not belong in the world of men.

Fire roared within the cracked opening of Hellgate, not the tame flickers of mortal flame but something alive and hungry. The heat radiating from its depths could have melted steel or turned bone to ash in an instant.

This was the gate to hell.

And standing at its edge, his massive claws dug into the trembling earth, was Adalward.

The golden dragon was a creature of impossible majesty. His four heads each bore horns that caught the sun and scattered it in dazzling arcs of light. His scales shimmered with the weight of millennia, glowing from within as though Heaven's essence had been woven into his flesh. His wings stretched wide, vast enough to blot out the sky, their membranes humming with power. For ages beyond counting, he had stood guard over this cursed place, a living barricade against the horrors that slithered below.

But something was different now.

The fire surged, twisting into shapes that should not exist. Faces with too many eyes, limbs that bent the wrong way, mouths frozen in silent screams. The air thickened, heavy with the stench of sulfur and rot. Adalward felt it before he saw it. The corruption seeped upward, tendrils of shadow snaking through the cracks, staining the world with their touch.

One of his heads lowered, nostrils flaring as embers spilled from between his teeth. A growl rose in his chest, deep enough to shake the desert floor.

Then a voice called his name.

"Adalward."

The sound was not a sound at all. It struck like a force, rattling the dragon's bones. It came from the pit, from the fire, from the darkness that even flames could not touch.

Adalward did not flinch. "Satan," he rumbled. "Still as impatient as ever."

Smoke coiled upward, thick and choking, twisting into form. A figure emerged, taller than any man, carved from shadow and malice. Curved horns framed a face that was both beautiful and terrible, the kind that could lead nations to ruin with a smile.

Crimson eyes burned like dying stars, and the air crackled with restrained power.

Satan, the King of Hell, stood at the edge of his prison. The world trembled.

"I remind you, dragon," he said, his voice sharp enough to whip flesh from bone, "that Heaven knows I will return. Until the day their king comes to build his kingdom, I shall rule the earth."

Adalward's scales flared with golden light, pushing back the suffocating dark. "You are impatient. It is still years before your first demon is allowed to ascend."

Satan's laugh was jagged, scraping against the mind. "One demon?" he sneered. "Even one of mine is enough to crack this world."

"Which demon do you speak of?"

"Tynan." Satan's grin widened, revealing teeth like shards of glass. "Lord of Darkness and Chaos. He will open the way for my rule."

Adalward's growl deepened, shaking the desert itself. "Even Tynan is bound by Heaven's decree. There are rules. First Tynan. Then your others. Only then will you rise. And only when your reign is complete will the Son of God return."

Satan's eyes gleamed, cruel and delighted. "Ah, dragon, you still cling to hope." His words dripped with mockery. "But open your eyes. The world is already mine. Every war, every betrayal, every whisper of corruption is another thread in my tapestry."

Smoke shimmered, and visions unfolded. Cities burning, streets running red with blood. Brothers turning guns on one another. Businessmen draped in expensive silk while the starving clawed at their feet.

"See how they kneel before greed?" Satan murmured. "How they slaughter in the name of pride? They need no demons to teach them sin. They perfect it themselves."

Adalward's gaze held steady, though sorrow flickered in his golden eyes. "You exaggerate. For every heart that turns black, another remembers mercy. For every hand raised in violence, one reaches out in kindness."

"Kindness?" Satan's laugh scraped bone. "Kindness does not stop the tide. You speak of scattered embers, while I command the wildfire." The visions shifted. Crowds screaming for blood. Children taught to hate before they could read. Nations devouring themselves. "They choose me. Not in words, but in deeds."

Adalward's wings flexed, scattering divine sparks into the abyss. "And yet redemption is always one choice away. A thief returning what he stole. A soldier laying down his arms. A mother who starves so her child may eat. Quiet faith still endures."

Satan sneered. "Redemption? A lie to comfort the damned. Their souls are mine long before their last breath." His voice dropped to a razor's edge. "Why do you think Heaven stays silent? Even they see the inevitable."

For the first time, Adalward's growl carried fury. "Heaven's silence is not surrender. It is patience. The final battle is not yet written."

"Then let us write it now." Satan's grin split wide. "Tynan is but the first stroke. Watch your precious faithful break. Watch as their prayers turn to curses. And when the last light gutters out…" His form dissolved, seeping back into the Hellgate. "Remember that you were warned."

Silence followed, heavy and suffocating.

Adalward stood alone, the desert wind howling, carrying with it the echo of Satan's taunts. The visions had faded, but their weight pressed against his ancient heart. The darkness would come. It would test the world. It would try to drown every flicker of light.

But as long as one flicker endured, as long as one soul still reached for grace, good will win over evil.

The storm was coming.

But storms, too, must pass.

CHAPTER 1

The Unshifted

The heavy rain hammered against the arched windows of the Dragon Council's Hall, rattling the glass and drowning the silence inside. A television flickered to life at the far end of the chamber, its screen showing a solemn news anchor seated behind a polished desk, his voice steady and practiced with years of repetition.

"As the days draw nearer to the predicted three days of darkness, speculation continues to grow," he said, his eyes fixed on the camera. "Experts remain divided on whether this event is rooted in scientific fact or whether it is simply another doomsday prophecy."

The screen cut to a scientist explaining the sudden increase of solar flares and unusual activity from the Sun, suggesting that such disruptions could affect the Earth's magnetic field. Then another guest, a popular YouTuber, dismissed the claims with a grin, pointing to the 2012 Mayan apocalypse as evidence of how people always gave in to irrational fears.

When the anchor returned, his tone carried a weight that seemed heavier than his words. "With the Sun becoming more erratic, some say we cannot afford to dismiss it. For now, it remains a waiting game, as many continue to hope this is only another false alarm."

Mariah Mac Naught, Chief of the Dragon Council of the West, sat at her vast desk, watching the broadcast with an expression that revealed none of her thoughts. She wore flowing silver and indigo robes embroidered with the sigils of the Council, the fabric shimmering faintly in the lantern light. Her long silver hair was drawn into a single braid that fell over one shoulder, gleaming like spun metal. Yet, her fingers, tipped with long, painted nails, tapped against the wood with an impatience that betrayed her unease.

Her composure was famous within the Council, her authority rarely questioned, yet even she could not entirely conceal the tension in her jaw as the storm outside pressed against the windows. Rain streaked the glass like silver threads, and the darkness of the night seemed to thicken as the storm rolled over the city. Lightning burst across the sky in sharp flashes, illuminating the office briefly and then plunging it back into darkness.

She reached for the remote and switched off the television, but the words lingered in the air, heavy as stone. She knew the prophecy. The three days of darkness. The arrival of Tynan. The world, and the dragons with it, stood on the edge of something far worse than anyone dared to admit.

The doors opened quickly and a thin secretary in a well-fitted three-piece suit stepped in, clutching an iPad. He hurried to the desk, his shoes clicking softly against the marble floor, and handed it over.

"I hope the list is ready, Mr. Fehmasus?" Mariah asked, extending her arm without hesitation and sliding the device from his grasp.

Fehmasus leaned over her shoulder, pointing to the screen with a finger that trembled slightly. "Only three, first dragon-born young adults, remain unshifted. They are between sixteen and seventeen. And one is..."

"The Chief of Drakon Academy's son, Tariel Fenwick," Mariah cut in sharply. Her eyes narrowed as she flicked to the boy's profile. "If he is under our roof, then we can keep him under watch."

The screen filled with Tariel's face. A tall, broad-shouldered young man with unruly dark hair that curled faintly at the ends. His brown eyes, thoughtful and brooding, seemed older than his years, and his jaw carried the strength of his father's bloodline. There was something calm about him, but it was not the calm of peace. It was dangerous, the quiet restraint of someone holding back more than he revealed.

"He looks like his father," Mariah murmured. "And dangerously calm. Inform Chief Decimus Fenwick to enroll him in the Academy without delay. It is any moment now. He is close to shifting."

Fehmasus nodded and swiped to the next profile. A girl appeared on the screen, the poor resolution of the camera unable to hide the sharpness of her gaze. Her long black hair fell untidily over her shoulders. Her green eyes glowed faintly, and behind her, the cramped kitchen looked broken and tired.

"She is a late bloomer as well. Everin Haydon," Fehmasus said, his voice curling with disdain. "She lives in Midows, New York. Second-hand clothes. A family of five. Two younger siblings. A mother who is a stay-at-home alcoholic. A father who drives trucks for Dragon's Bricks, never around, barely involved."

Mariah studied the image for a long moment. Despite the broken walls behind her and the untidy clothes on her frame, the girl's green eyes unsettled her. They were not the eyes of a helpless child. They were the eyes of still water hiding dangerous depths. "She will be sixteen soon. Perhaps she already feels it," Mariah said quietly. "Keep watch." She swiped again.

"And this," she said, her voice heavier, "is the most difficult one. The Bevington girl."

Phoenix Bevington's photo filled the screen, the polished lighting making her appear as if she had stepped out of an advertisement. Her golden blonde hair was cut perfectly, just above her shoulders, and curled at the ends. Her lashes were thick with mascara, and her lips were lined in an expensive shade. She wore a designer hoodie and branded jewelry, her pose set in front of a private gym. Even in stillness, her expression was one of pride, entitlement, and distance.

Fehmasus smirked. "And the hardest to bring to the Academy."

"But we must," Mariah said firmly, setting the iPad down with finality and rising to her full height. Her voice was steady and commanding, carrying the weight of the storm outside. "The end of times is approaching. If the two-thousand-year-old prophecy is true, if God is to return, then the demons will rise before Him. And the first will be Tynan, the Demon of Darkness and Chaos."

She turned toward the storm, her gaze fixed on the lightning that broke across the horizon, as though she could already sense something vast and ancient stirring in its depths.

"The truth is bitter. We must think of ourselves before He arrives. And the only way to do that," her voice dropped into steel, "is to kill the vessel that will allow the demon's return."

Fehmasus swallowed, the sound loud in the silence, but he did not argue.

"Send out the Dragon's Summon to the three families," Mariah commanded, her eyes unblinking.

Fehmasus hesitated, his voice quiet. "But the Dragon's Summon is a high-order directive, reserved only for shapeshifters of rank..."

Mariah turned her gaze on him, cold as iron. "The Council rules the West. Follow my order now."

CHAPTER 2

Shattered Reflections

Side-stepping a couple of homeless individuals, Everin Haydon walked cautiously through the slippery and dark alleys of Midows. She carried a bag full of groceries and she was late. Her younger siblings would already be back from school, and there was nothing in the fridge for them to eat. Her mother, as usual, would be lying on the sofa, scrolling through television channels in her half-drunken state.

She hurried up the narrow stairs to their cramped two-bedroom apartment. The stench of booze, cigarette smoke, and leftover food scraps rotting in the nearby flooded bin filled her nose, but she was used to it by now. This was the normal smell of her neighborhood.

Before she could unlock the door, her younger brother Samuel's scream pierced the air. "You ate all of it, Doriya!" His thirteen-year-old voice cracked with anger.

Any moment now her mother would explode. Beth Haydon's stern voice was known throughout Midows, and Everin knew it would terrify Samuel. She twisted the stuck key as fast as she could and yanked the door open.

Beth's yell blasted through the entrance.

"Get the hell out of my house, you son of a freak!"

Everin rushed inside and slammed the door before the annoyed neighbors came to complain. Samuel darted behind her just as Beth charged toward him with an empty alcohol bottle clutched in her hand.

Doriya stood frozen in the kitchen, her scream echoing through the apartment.

"Mum," Everin said firmly, planting herself between Samuel and Beth.

Beth swayed, her eyes bloodshot and unfocused, but her rage did not falter. "Come here, you brat. I'll spank your bottom red today!"

For a heartbeat, she hesitated when she recognized Everin. Then, with a violent cry, she smashed the bottle against the wall just behind Samuel. Shards rained to the floor, the sharp crack echoing through the room.

Everin could feel Samuel trembling against her back, his fingers clutching tightly at her torn sweater. She set the heavy grocery bags on the counter and turned, pulling Samuel into her arms. "Are you hurt?" she whispered, glaring over his head at Beth.

Samuel shook his head side-ways quickly. "I'm hungry. I just wanted to make some noodles. Doriya wanted to make some too. Then the stupid bowl dropped on the floor and Mum woke up."

Doriya, barefoot and edging carefully around broken ceramic pieces, shouted, "It wasn't me!"

Everin sighed. "Be careful around the shards, Doriya."

Beth staggered back to the sofa, muttering angrily. "I can't even rest in my own house. All this fuss over a bowl. Useless." She slumped heavily onto the cushions, rubbing her forehead.

Although Samuel was her younger brother, Everin had raised him like a mother, the same with Doriya. Protecting them was second nature, even if it meant standing against Beth herself. "It's fine. I'll make dinner soon. Go shower," she urged Samuel, pushing him gently toward the bathroom.

He hurried into their shared room, but before the door shut, Doriya shrieked, "Get out of my room!"

Everin followed, her patience thin. "Doriya, this is our room. Stop chasing Samuel out."

"But it's a girl's room. I want to make my videos, and he's annoying. You promised he'd move soon."

"Yes, he will. He'll move to the living room when we make space. For now, you'll have to share." But Doriya was no longer listening.

Everin left her, turning back to the kitchen. She unpacked the groceries and began cooking. At least tonight there would be meat because it was payday. A cashier's wages were small, but she made them stretch. Their father's money, wired from long truck hauls for Dragon's Bricks, was never enough once Beth had her share. It was her mum's alcohol that swallowed what little extra there might have been.

For now, Beth had collapsed on the sofa again, dozing in and out. Everin glanced at her and wondered, not for the first time, what tomorrow would bring. She hoped her dad would be home in two days, just in time for her sixteenth birthday. She would talk to him then.

The following day, Everin walked into her school, which offered no escape.

She attended a low socio-economic high school close to home, juggling part-time shifts and lessons, homework and housework. She wished she could move out, but Samuel and Doriya anchored her. Besides, she was only sixteen. Her father's words stayed with her: Everin, my mighty little dragon warrior, you know your mum can't do this. Please, look after your brother and sister. Keep them safe, will ya?

She had promised him. "Yes, Daddy. I'll do my best."
Now she wondered if she could keep that promise.

She walked into the schoolyard, and her breath caught. Jackson Miller, tall, handsome, captain of the basketball team, emerged from the building. The reason she never skipped class. He always walked with his friends, a group of equally attractive seniors, but Everin only had eyes for Jackson.

Her life allowed little room for friends. Between work, studies, and caring for her siblings, she was a loner. She admired Jackson from afar, never daring to speak.

Then fate intervened.

The basketball sailed through the air toward her.

Thud.

Her body froze. Time slowed. The ball streaked toward her face.

But a hand shot out, snatching it inches away.

Tariel Fenwick, Jackson's teammate, stood before her. Tall, broad-shouldered, his dark hair unruly yet striking, he held the ball with effortless strength. His deep brown eyes caught hers, alive with mischief.

"You should've dodged," he teased with a crooked smile. "Wouldn't want your pretty face smashed, would we?"

Everin blinked, stunned not only by the near miss but by him. He was close, so close she caught the scent of pine and warm leather. Her breath hitched.

She had always admired Jackson, the star, the golden boy. But Tariel's presence was different. It wasn't admiration. It wasn't daydreams.

It was a feeling. Immediate. Unexpected. Alive.

"Uh… thanks," she stammered, fumbling for words as her fingers brushed his while taking the ball. A shock raced up her arm.

"Anytime," Tariel said softly before jogging back, throwing her a wink over his shoulder.

Everin stood frozen, her thoughts loud yet blank. She should be thinking about Jackson. Instead, her pulse thundered with the memory of Tariel's fingers and the heat in his smile.

One day later, Beth announced that Marcus Haydon was coming home the following day. For once, the house stirred with excitement. Even Beth moved about more than usual, helping in the kitchen.

Everin wondered why he usually wasn't home like normal dads, and why he chose to work at Dragon's Bricks, so far away from home? Was this the reason Beth drowned herself in bottles of alcohol instead of being a good mum? She brushed the thought aside. Tomorrow would be better.

That night, sleep did not come easily. Everin tossed in tangled sheets, sweat clinging to her skin though the night was cold. Dreams pressed against her mind, thick and heavy. She heard whispers, faint at first, then sharper, like claws dragging against stone. A call. A command. A voice rising out of shadows she could not see.

Her chest tightened as if something inside her wanted to answer.

She gasped awake.

The room was dark and stifling. Her heart hammered so loudly she thought it would wake Samuel and Doriya. She pushed the blankets aside and stood on shaking legs, every step unsteady as though the floor tilted beneath her.

The bathroom door creaked open.

A single bulb flickered to life above the mirror, humming faintly. She stepped closer, her reflection staring back through the wavering glass.

For a moment, it was only her. Pale, tired, with dark hair sticking to her damp forehead.

Then the image shifted.

Her breath caught.

The left side of her reflection blurred, as though the mirror it-self could not decide what it was showing. Her skin darkened, black scales faintly visible beneath the light. A shimmer of green lit her eye, sharp and unnatural, glowing like a predator in the dark.

She reached up, trembling fingers brushing her cheek. Tough, scaly skin met her touch.

Everin gasped and stumbled back, as her pulse roared in her ears.

For a heartbeat, the reflection seemed to smile at her with something that wasn't her own face.

And then it was gone. Her skin felt smooth.

Only a girl stood there again, wide-eyed and horrified.

But there was no denying what she had just seen in the mirror. Partial, fractured, yet unmistakable. A creature she had only read about in books. And it had stared back at her... a dragon.

CHAPTER 3

The Truth Beneath the Skin

Night had fallen heavy over the Haydon household, pressing shadows into the narrow streets of Midows. The rain had stopped, but the air still clung damp and thick, as though the whole world were holding its breath.

Everin sat curled on her bed beneath the covers, her heart pounding so hard she thought it might burst. Samuel and Doriya slept peacefully in their beds, their breathing soft and steady, unaware of the storm twisting inside their big sister.

She could not stop thinking about the bathroom mirror.

The reflection.

The thing that had stared back at her, part dragon, part nightmare, something that should not exist.

Now the world itself seemed louder, sharper, unbearable. She could hear the faint scuttle of a stray cat creeping across the fence outside, the low hum of a car engine two streets away, and the rasp of a stranger's cough drifting through the night.

Someone was smoking somewhere nearby. She could smell the acrid tang of it in her nostrils as if the cigarette burned right in her room. Every sound, every scent pressed against her senses until she wanted to scream.

"No, no, no, no," she whispered, clutching her head and pressing her palms to her ears, as though she could block the flood of impossible noises. "This isn't real. This can't be happening to me."

She sank deeper into her blanket, pulling it over her head like a shield. Her hands shook as she fumbled for her phone, opening the screen and typing frantically. Search after search: hallucinations, monsters, dragon face in the mirror. She scrolled, desperate for answers, desperate for something that explained away the terror.

But the reflection in the mirror would not leave her mind. Those scales, and that alien eye staring back. It was not normal. It was not human.

Her pulse thundered in her ears. She shut her eyes tight, whispering to herself over and over, "It isn't true. I'm normal. I'm normal. I'm normal."

And all the while, she forced her voice low, keeping her fear locked inside the cocoon of her blanket, because if Samuel or Doriya woke, she did not know how she would ever explain. The floorboards creaked in the hallway, slow footsteps drawing closer. She stiffened, clutching the blanket as though thin fabric could shield her. A knock followed, quiet but firm.

"Everin?" Her father's voice was deep and steady. "Can I come in?"

Her throat felt dry. She forced the words out. "Yeah. Sure."

Marcus Haydon stepped inside, the weight of the world on his tired shoulders. He looked like a man caught between two lives, one as a long-haul trucker with worn boots and a dusty shirt, the other something older, something she could not quite put a name to. Yet his eyes, warm and watchful, still carried the kind of love that made her chest ache.

He sat on the edge of the bed, careful not to wake Samuel and Doriya. "You doing alright?"

Everin shook her head quickly, pulling her knees close to her chest. Her voice broke as she whispered, "No. I don't even know what I am. Something is wrong with me."

Marcus leaned closer, his voice steady. "Nothing is wrong with you."

Tears burned her eyes. She buried her face in her hands, words spilling out between sobs. "I saw scales on my arm. And my eyes, they were green, glowing, not human. I looked in the mirror and I saw… I don't know what I saw, but it wasn't me. It was like some monster. Like a dragon." Her shoulders trembled. "Dad, this can't be real. I can't be real."

Marcus reached out and gently pulled her hands away from her face. His touch was firm, grounding, his voice quiet but certain. "Everin, listen to me. You are not a monster." He let the words settle, then added with the kind of calm that left no room for doubt, "You are a dragon."

She froze, the sobs catching in her throat. Her wide eyes searched his, desperate and frightened. "No. I'm just me. I can't be… how do you even know that?"

"I can sense it," Marcus said softly, brushing a strand of hair from her damp cheek. "I felt the dragon's aura in you as soon as I walked into the house. I thought the same thing when it first happened to me, until I shifted at twelve."

Her eyes shot to his. "Twelve?"

He gave a rueful chuckle. "Set the garage on fire. Your grandmother nearly disowned me. I thought it would happen to you at thirteen or fourteen, but when it didn't, I figured the dragon blood skipped you. It turns out you are just late. Very late."

Everin wrapped her arms around her legs. "I don't feel like a dragon. I just feel… broken."

"No, sweetheart," he said firmly. "You are not broken. You are rare. And the Council knows it."

He stood and motioned for her to follow. "Come on. We will talk properly. I will make you hot chocolate."

The living room was dim, the hum of the old refrigerator filling the silence as Marcus worked at the stove. He moved smoothly, pouring milk and stirring cocoa; this simple act steadied her amid the chaos.

Everin sat on the couch, her fingers tracing the frayed edge of a cushion. When he handed her the mug, she held it close, letting the warmth seep into her palms.

Marcus stayed at the window for a moment, staring into the dark. His voice dropped lower, as though the night itself might be listening. "We received something." He paused and added softly, "Something rare."

Her head tilted. "What is it?"

He turned, his expression unreadable. "A Dragon's Summon."

The words meant nothing to her, and yet they felt heavy. "Is that… bad?"

He smiled faintly, though his eyes betrayed unease. "It is an honour. Dragon's Summons are usually sent to high-ranking shifters, council members, and leaders. Not ordinary drivers like me. Which is why this is different."

"Why us?"

"Because of you." His gaze lingered on her face. "Tradition says the firstborn carries the strongest dragon blood. I thought it skipped you, but maybe the Council senses something. Maybe they believe your time has come."

Everin stared into her mug, her voice quiet. "But I already started. Didn't I?"

He nodded. "Yes. And that is a good thing. The Academy is where you belong now. They will teach you how to manage what is waking up inside you."

A silence stretched between them, filled only by the low hiss of rain against the windows. Finally, she asked, "Does Mum know?"

Sadness touched his face. "She does. I told her a few weeks after we had started dating. You know I couldn't hide this from her forever, and I didn't mean to. But by the time I had gathered my courage to tell her, she had already fallen in love with me, and she was carrying you. She chose to stay, even though she is a Non-Draco."

His gaze dropped to his hands. "At first, she was happy, even proud. But as the years passed, the truth wore on her. I am not a wealthy dragon, Everin. I am a worker dragon. Our kind use our fire to smelt ore in the mines, and the work keeps me away for weeks, sometimes months. Your mother never forgave me for not being there, for not giving her the life she wanted. And in time, she began to hate what I was."

Everin did not answer, but inside she heard the echo of Beth's cruel words. Freak.

After a moment, she forced herself to ask, "So… what do you look like? As a dragon. Have I ever seen you?"

Marcus raised an eyebrow, a faint smile returning. "Want the full reveal?"

She shrugged, trying to sound casual, though her pulse quickened. "Maybe."

"Brace yourself."

He stepped back, his body tensing. His skin rippled, shimmered, then with a sound like a gale tearing cloth, he shifted. Scales of burnished copper flared across his body, catching the dim light and glowing with molten fire. His form expanded, wings unfolding with a leathery snap, eyes burning with fierce amber light. His horns arched high and proud, and fire simmered at the edge of his breath.

Half of him filled the room, the other half crashed through the back window, tail knocking over a chair on the balcony.

Everin gasped. Then laughter burst out of her chest. "Dad! You broke the window!"

The dragon snorted, the sound rolling like a laugh.

She stepped closer, her hand trembling as she reached out. Her fingers brushed the warm, scaled surface of his snout. It was smooth and ridged, like ancient armor, humming with power beneath. She traced the bridge of his nose, awe rising in her chest. "You are… beautiful."

He lowered his massive head in acknowledgment.

Then the scales dissolved, the wings folded away, and Marcus stood human again. His clothes were back on while his hair was damp with sweat.

Everin tilted her head, curiosity flickering. "Dad… I've always wondered. How do your clothes come back? Shouldn't they rip apart when you change like that?"

Marcus chuckled, brushing dust from his sleeve. "That's the trick of Aegisweave. It's an enchanted fabric, stitched into what we wear. It stretches and reshapes with the transformation, then settles back when we return to human form. Without it, believe me, we'd be ruining wardrobes every day." He smirked. "Or walking around half-dressed."

Everin giggled, though her voice carried wonder. "You looked incredible. But I am still telling Mum you broke the window."

His grin was tired but warm. "She will not be surprised."

Her smile faltered. "When I saw myself, it wasn't like that. It was dark. Scales on my arm. A glimpse in the mirror. For a second… I saw a dragon's face. Just part of it. Like it was watching me from inside the glass."

Marcus sat again, his tone gentler. "That is how it begins. A flicker. A feeling. The more it comes, the stronger it gets, and what you saw was your dragon."

She looked down at her hands. "It was powerful. Scary. But I could feel it waiting. Like it has been there all along."

He placed his hand over hers. "Then it is time you learned how to face it. The Academy will help you do that."

Everin stared into the mug, her reflection rippling in the cocoa. The dragon stirred again, stronger this time. It was waiting. Watching. And she could no longer pretend it wasn't there.

CHAPTER 4

The Journey to Drakon Academy

The morning light crept slowly into the Haydon household, painting the living room in muted grays and soft golds. It was the kind of dawn that whispered of change, heavy with silence and cloaked in an air of finality.

Samuel and Doriya huddled by the broken window, their breath fogging the glass as they peered through the jagged frame.

"Maybe a raccoon tried to escape after stealing Dad's leftover chicken," Samuel suggested with all the seriousness of a detective.

"Or a mutant bird with terrible navigation skills," Doriya added, poking her head halfway out.

Everin walked in just in time to hear them, and she stifled a laugh as her eyes met her father's across the room. Marcus sat at the table with a mug of coffee in hand, his expression perfectly calm, as if a dragon-sized hole in the window was nothing out of the ordinary.

"Morning," he said casually.

Everin bit her lip, fighting the giggle that rose in her throat. Last night's revelation was still sharp in her memory. Her father's dragon form had filled the living room, evoking awe, fear, and his long tail, which shattered the window.

Then Samuel's gaze caught her bags by the door. His brow furrowed. "Wait… you're going somewhere?"

Doriya spun around, eyes wide. "You're leaving?"

Everin's smile faded slightly as she walked closer to them. "Yeah. I wanted to tell you both last night, but…" she glanced at their sleeping faces in memory, "you looked peaceful. I didn't want to wake you."

From her hoodie pocket, she pulled out two hand-stitched bracelets, rough but made with care. She placed them into their palms. "Here. To remember me by. I made them last night."

She had not slept at all. The thought of her reflection in the bathroom mirror and her father's words had kept her awake, her mind racing. The bracelets were her way of holding on to what mattered, a thread that tied her to home.

Doriya's eyes filled with tears. "You're leaving for some fancy school, aren't you?"

Everin hesitated, then nodded. "Yes. It's… a boarding school. Dad's company helps send kids there if they show some kind of potential. I got picked." The words felt strange on her tongue, but she decided against saying the real name. Drakon Academy would only bring questions she could not answer. She forced a smile. "Today's my birthday, and apparently I have to get there right away to keep my spot."

Samuel blinked in surprise. "You got a scholarship? That's kind of cool." He tried to smile, but his voice wavered. "Well, just don't forget us when you become all famous and important. By the way, happy birthday Everin."

Everin chuckled softly and pulled him into a hug. "Oh thank you and I'll never forget you. I'll text you all the time."

Beth's door creaked open down the hall. She stepped out in her robe, arms crossed, her face drawn in shadows of disdain. Everin met her gaze. For a heartbeat, she thought her mother's expression might soften, but the flicker of judgment in her eyes gave her the answer.

"She knows," Marcus murmured under his breath.

Beth's voice was cold and flat. "If you're going, then go. But don't come back with wings and fire breath expecting a welcome party."

Samuel and Doriya looked at each other, puzzled, but Everin chose not to explain. That would be for another day, perhaps when her father was ready. She only looked at her mother for a long second before whispering, "Please be more patient with them. They need you."

Beth chose not to reply and quietly returned to her room.

Marcus pressed a kiss to Doriya's hair, then to Samuel's head, before leaning down to peck Everin gently on her crown. His satchel was already slung over his shoulder.

"I have to head off too," he said quietly.

Samuel scowled. "You just got here."

Doriya crossed her arms. "Of course. You always have somewhere else to be."

Everin winced at their disappointed faces. This was how it had always been. Marcus Haydon, half-legend and half-stranger, slipping in and out of their lives.

The ride in the black SUV was quiet. Forest roads wound upward, twisting deeper into the mountains, each turn pulling them farther away from the crumbling apartment and closer to the unknown.

Everin pressed her palms against her knees, staring straight ahead. "Dad," she said softly, "what if I do not fit in? What if I am too far behind? I mean… I am sixteen. Am I going to be stuck with the youngest ones?"

Marcus gave her a quick glance before turning back to the road. "No. The Academy has its own way of doing things. The Juniors are thirteen and fourteen. That is when most kids first shift, but they still need training. Learning to stand on four legs without falling on your snout, how to spread your wings without smacking someone in the face, you know, things like that."

The driver, a broad-shouldered man with a grizzled jaw and twinkling eyes, chuckled. "Name's Callum, by the way. And your dad is right. The Juniors are a mess. You will hear more crashing into walls than actual flying."

Everin managed a nervous laugh. "So what comes after Juniors?"

"The Seniors," Marcus said. "Fifteen and sixteen. By then they should be able to fly straight, though some still zigzag like drunks."

Everin raised her brows. "And the top tier?"

"The Finals," Marcus replied. "Seventeen and eighteen. By then, they are well-trained and know the dragon world inside and out. Once they finish, they can choose their paths. Some join the dragon army, some the Council, others find work in dragon-run businesses. And some daring ones try living like humans, but the Council still keeps track of all dragons. It is their aura. They have ways of tracing it."

The SUV rattled on, filled for a while only by the hum of the engine and the steady sweep of rain across the windshield. Then Callum muttered, almost to himself, about dragons who had been alive centuries ago, still shaping the Council's decisions.

Everin's head snapped toward him. "Wait. Centuries? How long do dragons even live?"

Marcus's voice carried patience, but also weight. "Much

longer than humans. Two or three hundred years is common. Stronger dragons, with deeper bloodlines and better control of their energy, can live far longer. A thousand years is not unheard of."

Everin's eyes widened. "That is… insane."

"Not insane," Callum grunted. "Just rare. The stronger the dragon, the longer its life. Do not worry, you will still get wrinkles someday."

Everin blinked at him, then turned back to Marcus. "Dad… then tell me seriously. How old are you?"

Marcus's mouth curved into a rueful smile. "About sixty-five."

Her jaw dropped. "You look thirty-five. Maybe thirty-eight. Not a day older. And are you telling me Doriya, Samuel, and I are your only children? No previous marriages or kids?"

Marcus's eyes settled on hers. "You three are my only children." He sighed and added, "We live long, but we do not look it. We move from place to place, village to village, to keep suspicions down. That is why dragon communities stick together. It is easier to blend in with our own kind."

Everin hugged her arms across her chest, her thoughts tangled. "And Samuel and Doriya? Will they—"

"They may never shift," Marcus said gently. "Not every child does. The blood runs strongest in the firstborn, and that is you."

The SUV fell quiet again, save for the hum of the engine and the rain brushing the glass. The forest pressed closer as the road wound higher into the mountains, each turn pulling them farther away from Midows and deeper into the unknown.

Three hours slipped past with Marcus's steady answers and Callum's gruff interruptions, until finally Marcus pointed to a faded sign by the roadside. "Dragon's Bricks," he said. "This is where I work most of the time."

The car rolled to a stop.

Everin turned to him, confused. "Wait… you're not coming to the Academy with me?"

"I wish I could," he admitted. "But it's just up the mountain from here. You're almost there. You'll be okay." Marcus turned back to her with a look that was both tender and heavy. "And hey, I'm just a call away. Anytime."

They hugged tightly before he stepped out, and the SUV carried her on alone.

The rest of the drive unfolded like a dream. Mist clung to the treetops, the air alive with the scent of pine and something older, something ancient. The mountain loomed higher, the roads winding narrower, until at last, she saw it.

Drakon Academy.

A castle carved into the cliffs, towers rising like stone sentinels, its walls half-shrouded in mist and sky. Dragons wheeled in the distance, their wings glinting as they caught the sun, majestic and undeniable.

Everin leaned forward, her breath caught in her throat.

This was real.

CHAPTER 5

Drakon Academy

Mist clung to the mountaintop like a living veil, parting only when the black Academy vehicle pulled to a slow, deliberate stop. The mid-morning sun filtered through thinning clouds, casting golden shards across the cliffs, and there it was at last, carved into a rock like something from another world, the Drakon Academy.

"Welcome to Drakon Academy, Everin," Callum said, climbing out and circling around to her door. He gave her a knowing grin. "Told you it would look different once we reached the top."

Everin hardly heard him. Her pulse fluttered as she stepped out, her boots crunching against the gravel as the sight before her stole her breath. Spires rose into the sky until their tips vanished into mist. Dragons wheeled in the distance, their shadows sweeping across walls etched with ancient runes. The whole scene felt as if it had been drawn from a story older than memory itself.

The sunlight streamed boldly now, warming the stone in gold, while the air, sharp with pine, whispered of secrets waiting to be uncovered. The Academy seemed alive, its walls shimmering faintly with the old magic of dragons long gone.

Everin paused, the cold air brushing her skin. For the first time since learning about her true nature, she experienced a sense of peace. Yet beneath that calm stirred unease. She tugged at the hem of her jacket, acutely aware of her body, her difference. She wasn't tall or elegant, not like the kind of girl who looked like she belonged here. In a place so grand, she felt small, out of place, almost unworthy.

By now, Callum had set her suitcase beside her, but before Everin could reach for it, he raised a hand.

"Leave it," he said easily. "The griffon dragons will handle your bags. Trust me, they're better porters than I'll ever be."

Two bird-like shapes swooped down, their wings cutting through the thin mountain air in strong, steady beats. As they landed beside her, Everin's eyes widened. Each creature stood taller than her shoulder, their bodies a seamless blend of dragon and bird. Broad feathered wings folded neatly against scaled shoulders, and their sharp, hooked beaks gleamed like polished steel.

"What… are they?" Everin asked, her voice hushed with awe.

"Griffon dragons," Callum explained, as though it were the most ordinary thing in the world. "They're carriers, used across the regions. Strong, tireless, trained for precision, and between you and me, they fold socks better than most first-years."

With a swipe of its talons, a ripple of magic passed over her luggage. In an instant, her suitcase shimmered and vanished.

Everin stiffened, her mouth parting in alarm, but Callum chuckled, his voice low and reassuring. "Relax, kid. Your things aren't gone. Griffons are precise. By the time you get to your dorm, your clothes will be in the cupboards and your books lined up on the shelves. They've been doing this job longer than either of us has been alive."

The second griffon ruffled its feathers and let out a soft, throaty croon, as if to confirm the promise.

Callum smirked. "See? Even they're telling you not to worry. You'll get used to them quickly. Around here, griffons keep the place running. Deliveries, messages, hauling supplies across the cliffs. You name it, and they can do it."

Everin blinked, staring as the griffons spread their wings

again, preparing to vanish into the mist. She had never imagined dragons could be anything other than terrifying beasts or grand symbols of power. Yet here they were, creatures that worked like clockwork, quietly carrying the weight of everyday life in this strange, hidden world.

Her mind spun. If even the smallest details of life here, like suitcases and cupboards, were steeped in magic, then what else lay ahead? What other wonders would she stumble into before the day was over? The thought made her pulse quicken, part fear, part excitement.

For the first time since stepping out of the car, Everin thought: maybe, just maybe, she wasn't here by mistake.

"Hey, Everin!"

The familiar voice jolted her from her thoughts. She turned to see Tariel Fenwick jogging toward her. His dark hair caught the light, his smile relaxed but edged with nerves.

"Tariel?" she asked, surprised that a boy from her high school basketball team was here, of all places.

"Yeah, surprise," he said with a shrug. "They waited and waited for me to shift, you know how it is for firstborns. But it never happened. The Council told me I was a late bloomer.

Guess they gave up waiting and let me in anyway." He nodded toward the gates. "Want me to show you around? I've lived here most of my life, and it's easy for newcomers to get lost."

Everin blinked. "I didn't even know you were a dragon…"

His grin was sheepish. "Not exactly something you bring up in conversation." He tilted his head toward the entrance. "Come on. You'll see."

The gates opened as they approached, creaking on their hinges, and revealed a courtyard alive with students. Teenagers her age clustered in groups, laughing, talking, some moving with a confidence she couldn't fathom.

"I only got here yesterday," Tariel said, lowering his voice. "Every hallway looks the same. But you'll get used to it."

Everin's eyes roamed the sheer height of the stone walls, focusing on the symbols carved deep into them. "Is the whole school this… grand?"

"That's putting it lightly," Tariel chuckled. "It wasn't built for comfort. It was built to remind us of where we stand."

Inside, the corridors stretched endlessly, lit by chandeliers that swung gently from vaulted ceilings. The air carried the faint musk of something ancient, something unyielding. Everin let her fingers graze the tapestries as they walked, the fabric heavy with forgotten stories.

They emerged into an open courtyard where a crowd gathered around a bald man in a sharp dark suit. His grin was wide, his gestures almost theatrical.

"That's my father," Tariel murmured. "Decimus Fenwick. Chief Professor or the Headmaster here."

Everin's eyes flicked between the two. Same forehead, same unmistakable brown eyes.

"Yeah," Tariel admitted with a guilty smile, "he's my old man."

The professor noticed them immediately, broke off from his group, and strode toward Everin with arms spread wide. "Ah, Everin Haydon, a new student!" His voice boomed with practiced cheer. "Welcome to Drakon Academy. I hope you're ready for the most chaotic years of your young dragon life!"

Despite herself, Everin smiled. The man's comical exuberance disarmed her. He made the weight of this place feel a little lighter.

"My father definitely has got a way of making everything seem more... manageable," Tariel whispered to her, and Everin chuckled softly in response.

After a brief introduction, Decimus Fenwick waved them off, insisting they explore. Tariel led Everin through more hallways until they reached the girls' dormitory.

"Well," Tariel said with a grin, "this is it. Welcome to your new home. Good luck, Everin." He spun on his heel and left before she could think of a reply.

Everin clutched her letter, staring at the strange sequence, which reminded her more of a fighter jet's name than a room number: **3FS–17**. The letter included a list with photographs of two girls assigned to the same room, and as she tried to recall their names, her thoughts shifted again to the room number.

The Flame Tier system. Tariel had explained it earlier, walking her toward the dorms with that maddeningly casual stride of his. "The number shows your flame tier. One Flame means level one, still sparking. Two Flames means level two, finally steady. Three Flames… that's level three, that is, nearly ready for the Final Flight. The S stands for Senior, and the chamber number comes last."

She remembered the way his eyes had gleamed as he leaned

closer, lowering his voice before softly speaking. "But hey, no one says the whole thing. Everyone just calls it 3FS." His grin had curved wickedly. "Not like the usual womanisers' 'Fix, Fok, and Forget after Screwing' theory…" His brow had arched, his expression pure tease, "…ours is 'Fix, Fumble, Fly and Survive.'"

Everin had noticed the way he had changed the pronunciation of the rude 'f' word. Having grown up in the tough suburbs of Midows, Everin was accustomed to such vulgar language. Especially things got way more colourful when her mum, Beth, was in the mood for quarrelling with the neighbors. Despite exposure to foul language, Everin had gone red to the tips of her ears when she heard Tariel murmuring in her ear. She had instantly fanned her face with the folded letter.

Tariel had laughed, easy and warm. "Careful, Haydon. If you blush any harder, people will think you've already caught fire." His grin widened as he added with a wink, "Guess you'll be the top in the Third Flame category then."

Now, standing in front of the dorm door carved with **3FS–17** in glowing brass script, Everin felt the weight of the words again. Senior. Third Flame. She hadn't even shifted once.

How was she supposed to survive at the third flame when her fire hadn't even started?

Her hand trembled slightly as she reached for the door handle, the glow daring her to step through and prove she belonged. Taking a deep breath, she stepped in.

Inside, the room was spacious but tense, the kind of space where personalities had already drawn their boundaries. Two girls looked up.

Phoenix Bevington sat on her bed surrounded by glossy magazines and a mountain of cosmetics. Her golden-blonde hair gleamed, her makeup flawless, her smile polite but edged with disinterest. "Oh, another newbie," she said, tossing her hair back. "Hope you don't mind, but I need my space to film tonight. Social media doesn't wait for anyone."

At a desk sat Tariya Gratton, her face lit by the glow of a laptop. She glanced up once, eyes cool and detached. "Just don't bother me when I'm gaming," she said, turning back to her screen without another word.

Everin stood for a long moment, unsure how to answer. It was obvious these girls had carved out their own worlds. And here she was, the outsider, already unsure if she had the right to belong.

She just needed something to keep her occupied, then perhaps she would think less about her dragon school life.

Everin decided to keep herself busy, maybe by unpacking, but when she checked her cupboards, she realized the Griffon dragons had already organized her things with neat precision.

She picked up her phone and texted her dad and Doriya to let them know she was settled in at her new school campus.

One glance at Tariya and Phoenix, both absorbed in their devices, made Everin feel even more out of place. How could they sit there so calm while her own thoughts tangled in a storm of nerves and determination? She reminded herself firmly that Drakon Academy was her reality now, for better or worse.

And she would have to face it.

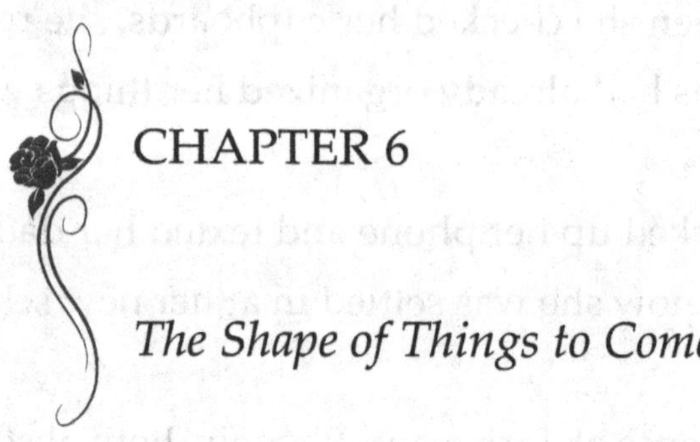

CHAPTER 6

The Shape of Things to Come

The dining hall was unlike anything Everin had ever imagined. It was vast, more like a grand hall than a simple dining space, set beneath soaring arched ceilings. Stained-glass windows bathed the chamber in rainbow hues as the morning light streamed through. Multiple long tables filled the room, crowded with students already deep in conversation over their meals. The air buzzed with chatter, a blend of excitement, nerves, and the familiar clamor that came with the start of the day.

At one end of the hall was a grand fireplace that crackled with warmth, a comforting contrast to the cold mountain air outside. On the walls, ancient tapestries hung, depicting dragons of all shapes and sizes, some majestic and others fearsome.

Everin grabbed a tray of food, an assortment of eggs, fruit, and some bread that smelled warm and yeasty, and took a seat near the end of one of the long tables. She wasn't sure who to sit with, so she took the seat furthest from the loudest groups of students. Her eyes scanned the room as she tried to get a feel for the place. One good thing about Drakon Academy was that she didn't have to worry about preparing or earning to put meals on her plate. She noticed Phoenix, her blonde room-mate, sitting with a few other students at a table nearby, clear-ly more interested in her phone than the food in front of her.

Tariel spotted her and waved from across the room. He was sitting with a group of students, some familiar faces from their arrival, and smiled brightly when Everin made eye contact. Everin nodded back, grateful for the familiarity, but her mind was already drifting to the upcoming lesson.

Today was the first day of class, and Everin could feel the weight of her dragon heritage pressing down on her, heavy and uncertain. How could she possibly learn how to shift, to control this power, when she still wasn't sure who she was?

"Everin!" Tariel called out, his voice cutting through her thoughts. "Come sit with us. We're about to head to class!"

She quickly grabbed her tray and joined him at the table. He was chatting with a couple of other boys, Rhodes and James, who both had an air of superiority about them. They were both muscular and seemed to be in their element in the Acad-emy, their casual sneers directed at the students around them.

Given her introverted nature, Everin couldn't even talk to the two boys apart from a few shy, monosyllabic replies.

As they finished their meals, the bell rang, signaling that it was time for class. Everin's stomach fluttered, but Tariel offered a reassuring smile. "Shapeshifting class. Perhaps they'll do some magic and turn me into a dragon today!" joked Tariel, then asked calmly, "You ready?"

"Not at all," she muttered, but her voice held a trace of humor.

The classroom was massive, almost as grand as the dining hall, with enormous windows letting in the soft morning light. The walls were lined with shelves filled with books, scrolls, and relics, many of which seemed to have a connection to dragons and their powers. The center of the room was cleared, leaving plenty of space for students to stand in a group. At the front of the room, a tall woman stood waiting for them, her posture stiff with a no-nonsense attitude. Professor Abagail Stark, the Shapeshifting instructor, was a striking figure who looked like she was in her early thirties, tall, with sharp features and an air of authority that immediately silenced the room.

"Good morning," she said, her voice firm but controlled. "I

trust you all are ready to begin your lesson in shapeshifting. For some of you, this will be your first attempt. For others, it is a chance to sharpen what you already know. Either way, this will not be easy. Shapeshifting demands focus, discipline, and above all, control."

Professor Stark stepped to the center of the training hall, her heels clicking sharply against the stone floor. "Steady your breath," she instructed, voice calm yet firm. She inhaled deeply, then let her body flow with it. "Focus on the rhythm. Let it guide you." Scales rippled across her skin, bronze and glinting in the sunlight. Her frame stretched, bones reshaping with a sound like bending timber, wings unfurling in a powerful sweep that stirred the air. In the space of a heartbeat, a sleek dragon stood where she had been, her eyes glowing with a calm, unshaken fire.

She lowered her head, exhaled a controlled plume of smoke, then shifted back with the same precision, her robes settling neatly around her as if untouched. Her face betrayed no strain, only expectation.

"That is what control looks like," she said, her gaze sweeping over the class. "The breath anchors the shift. In through the nose, steady and deep, and with the release, you allow the dragon within you to rise. But without control, you will stumble and lose yourself."

Her eyes lingered on the nervous faces in the front row, then hardened slightly. "Now… let us see what you can do."

A few students in the circle shifted nervously on their feet, but Professor Stark was unmoved by their discomfort. She raised an eyebrow. "Each of you will attempt to shift into your dragon form. Focus on your connection to your inner dragon and the elements you are closest to."

Everin took a deep breath. She was terrified, terrified of failing, terrified of what might happen when she finally tried to shift. Her hands trembled, but she stood up along with the others.

"Let's begin with Tariya," Professor Stark said, pointing to the quiet girl standing at the right end of the group. Tariya took a few steps forward, her face unreadable as she closed her eyes and took a deep breath. A moment later, a ripple of energy passed through her, and to Everin's shock, Tariya's form shimmered, her body becoming translucent as she shifted into a sleek, silver-scaled dragon with glowing eyes.

The students gasped, and even Professor Stark allowed herself a small smile of approval. "Impressive," she said coolly. "But not perfect. You must learn to maintain your form without distraction."

Tariya gave a small shrug and shifted back into her human form, clearly pleased with herself.

"Next, Miss Bevington," Professor Stark called, turning her gaze to Phoenix, who was standing slightly apart from the group, staring at her phone.

Tariel whispered in Everin's ear, "Hmmm, a Bevington is amongst us."

"Should I know the Bevingtons? She's my roommate and a total social media freak," Everin pursed her lips, uninterested in others. She wanted to focus on herself.

Rhodes, who was next to Tariel, drawled, "Bevingtons are the richest dragon family on earth. Most of the mining companies belong to them."

Everin had always known she understood little of the dragon world, but only now did she grasp the true depth of her ignorance.

Phoenix Bevington didn't look up as Professor Stark called her name, but after a beat, she sighed dramatically and shoved her phone into her pocket.

"Fine," she muttered, rolling her shoulders before shutting her eyes. Nothing happened. "See? No matter how hard I try, nothing happens. And honestly, why should I care? I already know I can't transform, and even if I could, what's the point? I don't need a dragon form. My family's rich. It's not like I'm ever going to smelt ores in the mines my family owns or play combat for the Council."

She gave a heavy shrug, as if that settled the matter, then sauntered toward the windows. Pulling out her phone again, she angled it for the best light, already more interested in snapping selfies with the forest backdrop than in proving anything to Professor Stark.

Some students oohed at her instant defiance, but Professor Stark wasn't someone to let go easily.

"Phoenix!" Professor Stark's voice cut through the air like a whip. "This is not the time to focus on social media! You are here to learn control, not to take selfies."

Phoenix rolled her eyes and reluctantly put her phone away. "I'll work on it," she said with a shrug, clearly uninterested.

Professor Stark gave her a piercing look. "I expect better focus from you, Phoenix Bevington. Meditation is your next task. Focus on your breathing and your connection to your dragon.

Do it now, or I will not hesitate to confiscate that phone and send you to the meditation chamber."

Phoenix's lips pressed into a thin line, but she nodded. "Fine," she muttered, sinking into a cross-legged position on the floor.

Next, it was Tariel's turn. He stood up with an expression of determination, but when he closed his eyes and focused, nothing happened. He tried again, his brow furrowing, but still no transformation came. The other students shifted uncomfortably, and a few chuckled quietly under their breath.

Rhodes sneered from the back of the room. "Nice try, Fenwick. Looks like your dragon's still on vacation."

James snickered beside him. "Maybe he's too weak to shift. Maybe he's not even a dragon."

Then a voice cut through from the back. "Seventeen and still with the Seniors," sneered Calder Vane, a tall boy with sharp features. "Should have been a Final by now. Guess you're just broken."

A ripple of laughter spread until Professor Stark's voice cracked like a whip.

"Vane." Her eyes snapped to him, cold as steel. "Since you

have energy to waste on insults, you will demonstrate a full transformation. Now. And you will hold your dragon form through the rest of this lesson until I say otherwise."

The smirk drained from Calder's face. He stood reluctantly, muttering under his breath as the laughter around him died into uneasy silence.

Tariel's fists unclenched slightly, though the flush remained on his cheeks. Everin could feel the tension shifting in the room, the weight of every eye on both boys now.

"Keep trying, Fenwick," Professor Stark said again, her voice steady but unyielding. "Your first shift is always the hardest."

Finally, it was Everin's turn. Her heart hammered against her ribs. For a moment, she wished she could disappear into the crowd and become invisible among the others. She had no idea how to command the storm inside her, how to shape it into something she could control. But then she thought of her father, of the way he had believed in her when she could not believe in herself. Shifting was not just about proving she belonged here. It was about survival. It was the only way to claim her place in this dragon world. And more than anything, she wanted to prove to him and to herself that she could.

She closed her eyes and focused, imagining the power coursing through her veins, the massive dragon she was destined to become. She pictured the scales, the sharp claws, the burning fire inside her chest, and willed it to happen. For a moment, nothing stirred. Then, as if struggling against an invisible barrier, a few dark scales began to shimmer faintly across her arms and shoulders. They appeared one by one, scattered and uneven, like fragments of a broken puzzle. The transformation stopped there, her skin tingling with the sensation, but nothing more. It wasn't what she had hoped for. There were no powerful wings or roaring dragon, but it was at least something. She let out a shaky breath, disappointed yet relieved that she hadn't failed completely.

Professor Stark, who had been watching closely, stepped forward with a measured tone. "It's a start, Everin," she said, though her voice was firm. "You've joined us in the middle of the year, and there is much for you to learn. Shapeshifting takes time, especially when the nature of your dragon form is... complex." She turned to Phoenix, then to Tariel, both of whom were doing no better. "You, too, have a long way to go. The process is slow, but persistence is key."

But even as she stepped back into the line of students, Everin felt the strange truth pressing at her chest. Whatever slept inside her was not meant to stay hidden for long.

CHAPTER 7

Sparks in the Stacks

It was their second lesson of the day, Dragon History. Everin sat at the back of the class, a little uneasy but trying to focus on Professor Edna Graeves, who stood in front of a large smart interactive board filled with images of various dragon species. Today's topic: Rare Dragons. As she listened to the professor's deep, authoritative voice, Everin felt a strange mix of curiosity and dread. She had no idea what kind of dragon she might be, let alone if she was even capable of shapeshifting yet.

Professor Graeves began by explaining the smallest and most elusive of dragons, the Minutez, a species so tiny that it could fit in the palm of a hand, barely noticeable in the wild. Everin's mind briefly wandered, imagining such a small creature existing in a world full of enormous, terrifying dragons.

Just then, a chubby teen, Garry Goldwin, commented, "Minutez is best suited to be a pet for daddy's girl." He sourly eyed Phoenix Bevington, the wealthy princess in the Academy, while some students laughed.

"Big dragons are good for one thing: working in the mines. I'd rather be a pampered pet than smelt ores every day!" This time, Phoenix ended up jabbing a lot of poor and middle-class dragons in the classroom.

However, Professor Graeves, walking between the student desks, intervened smoothly, "The Minutez is capable of entering places that normal dragons can't enter, apparently due to its size, and it can also burn holes in the palms of an enemy. Basically, we all have our strengths and weaknesses, which brings us to the most dreaded dragon." The professor's tone shifted, becoming more ominous as she mentioned the three-headed Hell's Fire Dragon.

James asked doubtfully, "I thought hell was just a cuss nowadays."

Rhodes and others joined the fun as he mouthed behind the professor, "Freaking hell!"

Immediately, Professor Graeves turned, with flowing yellow fiery eyes as she brought her now scary face near Rhodes and asked menacingly, "One way to find out if hell exists or not is to die."

Rhodes turned white as a sheet of paper, and he immediately mumbled, "I'm sorry, Professor."

"If Hell exists," Professor Graeves continued, pacing the front of the class, "then so must Heaven. The Hell's Fire Dragon and the Divine Dragon, the Guardian of Hell's Gate, are the stuff of legends or religions. We have no confirmed sightings of these creatures for thousands of years, but ancient religious texts have always mentioned them. Dragons are as old as religion itself. While many consider us to be mythological, our existence is proof that what the old scriptures say about gods and demons is more than mere stories."

Everin shifted uncomfortably in her seat, trying to wrap her mind around the possibility that she could be connected to such unknown, legendary forces. Beside her, Tariel, who had been silent through most of the lecture, looked just as intrigued, though it was clear from his relaxed posture that he wasn't as overwhelmed by the subject. Phoenix, on the other hand, appeared completely uninterested, scrolling through her phone, probably checking her social media as usual.

Before Everin could fully digest the weight of Professor Graeves' words, one of the more nerdy students in the front row, Ameera Morgraff, raised her hand, eager to make her mark. "That's because Heaven and Hell don't actually exist," she said, her voice husky and slightly smug. "We live in a simulation."

The classroom fell silent for a beat before Professor Graeves responded, her eyes narrowing slightly. "And who created that simulation? Dragons are as old as time, and so are religions. Generally speaking, the five major religions in the world all have these commonalities: a Supreme Being, the presence of heaven and earth. Whether or not you believe in Heaven and Hell, our very existence is proof that these ancient scriptures hold some truth. Dragons, gods, demons, these are not just stories, Ameera." She paused, letting the words sink in. "For many millennia, dragons like us have lived in the shadows of those myths. But this is not the Ancient History of Dragons lesson, and you are here to learn that dragons are not just fairy tales. We are flesh and bone, with power beyond comprehension."

A collective groan rippled through the classroom as Professor Graeves handed out the assignment for the day: a three-page paper on the rare dragons mentioned in the lesson. She added as students passed her, "Don't worry, you all have free periods because your professor for Dragon Combats is on leave this week, so you have plenty of time."

Everin could hear some of the other students whinging, clearly not thrilled about the additional work. Phoenix muttered under her breath, "I don't even know where to start with that," while Tariel simply gave her a small, understanding smile.

Everin, despite her growing anxiety about what she might discover about herself, pulled out her notebook. She wasn't sure she was ready to confront the truth of her dragon nature, but she couldn't back down from this. Not now. As she scribbled down the last few notes on Rare Dragons, she couldn't help but wonder, what kind of dragon was she?

The towering, ancient building loomed in front of Everin, its stone façade covered in ivy that seemed to weave and crawl over every inch of the structure. The large, carved wooden doors were open, and the sign above the entrance read, ***Dragon's Abode of Literature***. Everin stood, furrowing her brows for a moment, unsure whether she was at the right place or not. She surely wanted to go to the library, not to some dragon's abode.

"Bit archaic, I guess," Tariel said from beside her, a grin on his face as he saw her hesitating. "But it's the library for us, and believe me, people can get even lost in there."

They entered the library, passing through a few desks and a couple of students busy with their work.

"Did you say we can get lost here?" she asked Tariel sarcastically, nodding at the almost empty space.

"It's too early to judge yet, Miss Haydon," Tariel drawled as he walked backward ahead of Everin, giving her a full dose of his charming smile full of secrecy.

Finally, they reached the counter, where a woman who looked like she was in her fifties, with a witch-like hairstyle that looked like a pointed hat, was sitting behind a desk reading a thick, dusty book. She glanced up at them over the top of her glasses with a mix of indifference and a slight sense of annoyance.

"Ah, Mr. Fenwick," she said with a sigh. "I see you've brought another one."

Everin tilted her head. Another one? So this was not the first time Tariel had helped. She had thought his kindness was only for her, but now she realized it was part of him, and somehow that made her feel safer by his side.

The librarian looked at Everin, her gaze lingering for a second longer than necessary. "Since you can't transform yet, you'll need the Imprint of Dragon's Blood."

Everin blinked, confused. "Imprint of Dragon's Blood?"

The librarian rolled her eyes dramatically, clearly not bothered by the question. "It's like a passkey," she explained, her tone irritated. "You can't go flying through the air and land on top of the bookshelves like other students. But I suppose I'll trust Mr. Fenwick to explain it to you."

She reached into her desk drawer and pulled out a shimmering dragon's scale, handing it to Everin. The scale was smooth and cold to the touch, its surface gleaming with a shimmering glow. Tariel gave a playful bow as he took another scale from the librarian.

"Will do, Madame Corvella," he said with a grin, making Everin chuckle despite the awkwardness of the situation.

He led her through giant metal doors inside, and she followed him into what seemed like an entirely different world.

"W... ow..."

Everin steadied herself as she stood at the edge of what appeared to be a massive rocky hollow. Definitely larger than a football field.

The library was a cathedral of knowledge. A vast open floor stretched out before them, dropping in tiered levels like a stadium carved into the mountain itself. The air was rich with the scent of parchment, ink, and old enchantments. It felt more like an enchanted amphitheater than a traditional library.

Dragons, sleek and majestic, flew through the air, gliding silently between towers of books. Some carried scrolls or tomes in their claws, while others simply observed from above, their glowing eyes scanning titles as if judging their worth.

Tariel pointed upward. "Smaller dragons fly in between the aisles or lower levels, but the big ones," he paused as a massive, horned dragon soared above, its wings stirring a gust that ruffled Everin's hair, "mostly stay near the tower tops. Any lower, and they might knock over a shelf or two. And trust me, Madame Corvella would breathe fire herself if that happened."

Students in human form sat at desks below, scribbling notes or chanting softly from open grimoires. Every tower-sized bookshelf had its own spiraling ramp, and delicate ladders leaned precariously along their sides. Crystal lanterns hovered mid-air, casting golden pools of light on reading alcoves and crannies. Arcane symbols shimmered faintly along the bannisters.

"You see this barrier?" Tariel asked. "To pass it, you either need to be in your dragon form or have the passkey."

When she stepped through the barrier, it felt like dipping through a layer of cool mist, tingly, slightly pressurized, and oddly invigorating. On the other side, the air smelled more potent, filled with crackling energy and the hum of magic.

Tariel led the way down a winding staircase carved into the wall, their steps echoing lightly in the vastness. Partway down, they reached a circular platform with a brass pole in the center.

"This is the quick drop," Tariel said casually, just as the platform clicked.

"Wait, the wha—"

Suddenly, the platform dropped.

Everin shrieked and instinctively grabbed onto Tariel's jacket, yanking it off his shoulder. Her fingers curled tightly around the thick fabric, pulling it down and exposing his sculpted bicep.

Tariel chuckled under his breath but said nothing. He steadied himself by gripping the pole with one hand and looped the other arm firmly around Everin's waist.

She slammed into his chest with a muffled gasp, her cheek

brushing against the crook of his neck. The scent of cedar, fresh spice, and something uniquely him filled her senses. Her lips accidentally grazed the warm skin just below his jaw. Her palm flattened against warm, solid strength.

Her eyes widened. She froze.

"You okay?" Tariel murmured, his voice tinged with teasing amusement.

Everin pulled back slightly, flustered. "Um... I think I just kissed your neck. Sorry."

His eyes twinkled. "Well, that's one way to make an impression."

Her blush deepened.

The platform slowed, hovering a few feet above the ground before gently coming to a stop. Tariel helped her off, his hand still lightly on her back.

"You've got..." she gestured vaguely toward his neck. "Lip gloss. Right... there."

He smirked. "Good. Now I've got a souvenir." The rogue didn't bother to wipe it off.

She rolled her eyes, but her heart was thundering.

They stepped forward into the lowest tier of the grand library, surrounded by magic, mystery, and the beginnings of something neither of them could quite name yet.

As they made their way deeper into the library, Everin spotted Tariya sitting at a table in the back, hunched over a laptop, her fingers flying over the keyboard. She appeared completely absorbed in what she was doing.

Everin made her way over, Tariel following closely behind. As she approached, she noticed Tariya was using a small device with a scanner attachment.

"I thought it wasn't possible to scan dragon scriptures," Tariel remarked, raising an eyebrow as he peered over Tariya's shoulder.

Tariya smirked, looking up at him. "It wasn't... until my uncle got his hands on a special scanner from the black market. It can translate the language of Dracos into English. Saves a lot of time."

Everin raised an eyebrow. "Wait, so you've been scanning all these books?"

"Yep," Tariya replied nonchalantly. "You wouldn't believe how much useful information is here. I'm just looking for some of the older texts about the Hell's Fire Dragon."

Just then, she paused and squinted at Tariel's neck.

"Uh, Tariel," she said slowly, smirking. "Is that… lip gloss on your neck?"

Tariel gave her a look of mock horror. "What? I'm a marked dragon now."

Everin turned a shade redder and quickly buried her nose in the nearest book.

"You're blushing," Tariya teased.

"She's just admiring your tech," Tariel replied smoothly, taking a seat. "And maybe wondering if I taste like cinnamon."

Everin groaned. "Can we please talk about dragons instead?"

Tariya winked. "Only if you stop swooning and start reading."

Everin sighed, her shoulders slumping. "I can't even read Dracos… How am I supposed to understand all of this?"

Tariya grinned, tapping her device. "Don't worry. I've got you covered." She slid her scanner toward Everin. "Here, use this. It'll translate everything for you."

Everin reluctantly took the scanner and started looking through the book. Her fingers brushed against a large, ornate page, and she froze when she saw a picture of the Hell's Fire Dragon, its three heads glaring fiercely from the illustration. She couldn't look away. The eyes of the dragon seemed too familiar, too intense.

Everin's breath hitched, her heart suddenly pounding in her chest. The dragon's green glowing eyes were the same as the ones she had seen in the bathroom mirror, dark, terrifying, and full of an insatiable hunger. Her thoughts raced. Could it be…? Was she the one this dragon was tied to?

Her hands trembled slightly as she continued to read the page, her stomach tightening with a sense of dread.

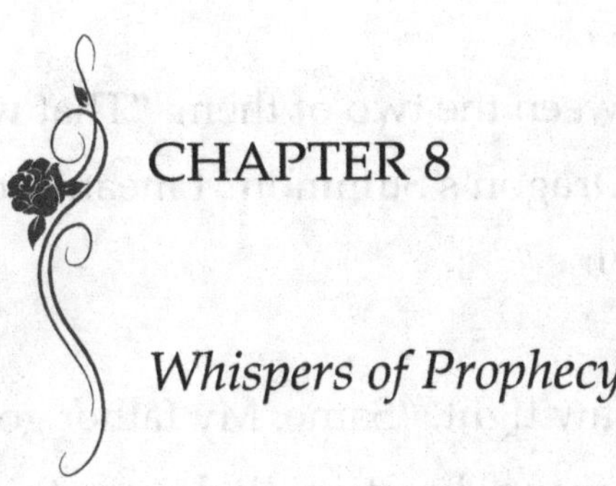

CHAPTER 8

Whispers of Prophecy

A few days after their trip to the library, Everin, Tariel, and Phoenix walked toward the lecture hall for their special class on the Language of Dracos. The air buzzed with quiet unease; none of them had fully shifted yet. Despite their progress and the knowledge they were soaking up at Drakon Academy, the sense of something unfinished clung to them all.

Phoenix was the first to break the silence. "Honestly, I still think the Council's watching us," she muttered, hugging her arms around herself. "Not just out of curiosity either. They're waiting."

Tariel arched a brow. "Waiting for what? For us to finally sprout wings and start breathing fire in our sleep?"

Phoenix didn't laugh. "Maybe. Or maybe they're tracking how we handle things, how long it takes, how we react. Like we're part of some long experiment."

Everin glanced between the two of them. "That would explain why they sent the Dragon's Summon? I mean… my dad got one, that's why I came."

Tariel nodded, his jaw tight. "Same. My father got one too. It wasn't a request; it was a directive. Pack your things. You're going."

Phoenix rolled her eyes. "Mine nearly threw the letter in the fire. Said the Bevingtons don't take orders. But in the end, they sent me. Couldn't risk defying the Council, could they?"

Everin rubbed her arms, feeling the breeze graze her skin. "But you've both known about dragons your whole lives. I only found out the night I partially transformed, and my dad showed up. I thought he was just late for my birthday, then boom, 'you are a dragon,' summon, Academy. It was all so fast."

"Yeah, that's the thing," Phoenix said, eyes narrowing. "Most dragon shifters transform in early adolescence, puberty, some-times younger. Twelve or thirteen, that's the usual age for first shift."

"And we're way past that," Tariel added. "I'm seventeen.

Phoenix is sixteen and a half, while you've just turned sixteen. That makes us... anomalies."

"Late bloomers," Phoenix supplied, tossing her hair back. "That's what they call us. Like we're a special category. Or a warning sign."

Everin studied Tariel out of the corner of her eye. He laughed lightly, brushing it off, but she sensed something beneath it. He might joke, but she could tell he would rather have been in the Finals, where seventeen-year-olds belonged. Instead, here he was, stuck among the Seniors, and pretending it did not sting. Still, she found herself liking the way he carried it with ease, turning embarrassment into something lighter.

Phoenix huffed. "Look, I'll be honest. I'm not exactly killing myself trying to shift. What's the point? I don't need to breathe fire to get through life. I'd rather spend my time doing my makeup, throwing parties, and living off my family's money. The heiress thing is way easier than turning into a flying lizard."

Everin couldn't help but laugh softly, even though she knew Phoenix meant every word.

As they walked, Everin's eyes drifted to the edges of the corridor. A pair of squat creatures shuffled past, no higher than her waist. Their bodies looked as though they had been carved from rough stone, thick arms dangling as if unused. From behind each of them trailed a ridged dragon tail that brushed the floor with every step, sweeping up dust in lazy arcs. Draggrels. That was what Tariel had called them earlier: half-troll, half-dragon creatures that made up the Academy's cleaning staff. One flicked its clawed fingers, and a quill that had rolled beneath a bench lifted into the air and zipped neatly into a student's satchel. Another scowled as it muttered a guttural spell, and the grimy streaks on a tall stained-glass window melted away like mist. They ignored the passing crowd completely, their stone faces twisted into permanent frowns, grumbling softly as they went about their chores. Watching them, Everin thought they looked both strange and ordinary at once, as if the magic of this school extended even to its janitors.

Everin's thoughts swirled. She hadn't known this. Her father had mentioned being late to shapeshift. He had emphasized that the Academy was the safest place for her now. But now it made more sense why he had looked so serious, so strangely urgent.

They walked in silence for a moment until Phoenix leaned closer, lowering her voice as if savoring her own words. "And then there's the prophecy. You've heard of it, right? The Feared One. Supposedly, there will be a dragon, who will be stronger than the rest, and is destined to bring ruin if not stopped."

Everin's brow furrowed. "The Feared One? What are you talking about?"

Phoenix's eyes glinted, pleased to be the one to tell her. "An old legend. A vessel for the demon Lord Tynan, the so-called demon of chaos and darkness. The prophecy says when the Feared One rises, the world burns." She gave a short laugh and waved her hand dismissively. "But come on, demons? In today's world? That's more fairy tale than fact. People whisper about it like it could happen, but it's the kind of story you tell to scare hatchlings into behaving."

Tariel didn't laugh. His tone was steady, matter-of-fact. "Maybe. But the Council doesn't dismiss it as a fairy tale. Why else do you think they care so much about anomalies? They might not say it aloud, but they believe in the prophecy. At least enough to keep watch."

A chill passed through Everin. "So you think that's why they're watching us? Because of this Feared One?"

"Maybe," Phoenix said with a shrug, though her bravado flickered.

Tariel's tone was firm, not unkind. "The Council keeps records of every dragon's aura. Think of it like a map. They know where dragons are, how many there are, and where the blood-lines run strongest. It helps them maintain balance. To make sure we don't cross the line with humans. To make sure no one dragon becomes too dangerous."

Everin shivered at the thought. The idea of being watched wasn't pleasant.

As they reached the steps of the lecture hall, she looked down at her hands, feeling the weight of it all. Special. Different. Watched. None of it felt comforting. More like a warning she couldn't yet decipher.

"What if we're not just here to learn?" she whispered, mostly to herself. "What if we're here because we're dangerous?"

Neither Phoenix nor Tariel answered. They didn't have to. The silence between them said enough.

Everin, Tariel, and Phoenix were seated in a small, sleek class-room, its walls lined with smartboards and polished desks. The air was filled with an expectant energy as they waited for their Language of Dracos lesson to begin. Tariel had his usual relaxed posture, leaning back in his chair with an air of casual confidence, while Phoenix sat upright, her eyes eager for what was to come. Everin fidgeted slightly in her seat, her hands nervously twisting the hem of her sleeve. This was a class she hadn't expected to be intriguing but was already looking forward to.

Just as the bell rang, the door to the classroom swung open, and in walked Mrs. Inkpen, the associate lecturer for the course. She was a middle-aged woman with sharp, focused eyes and an air of quiet authority. Her hair was pulled back into a tight bun, and her attire was impeccable, with a flowing scarf that seemed to move independently of her.

Trailing behind her was none other than Jackson Miller, the basketball hunk from Everin's school and her sweet crush. He flashed a grin as he entered, giving Tariel a fist pump as they exchanged a brief, familiar greeting. Jackson was tall, with broad shoulders and an athletic build, his presence almost magnetic. He effortlessly made his way to an empty seat next to Tariel, who waved him over.

"Yo, man," Tariel said, grinning as Jackson sat down next to him.

"Hey, Tariel. How's it going?" Jackson gave a quick wave to Everin and Phoenix, his smile infectious as usual.

Everin's heart skipped a beat, her cheeks flushing. She gave him a shy, almost timid wave, her excitement barely contained. Jackson had always seemed out of her reach, more of a figure in the background of her life than someone she could have a real conversation with. But here, in the Academy, things felt a little different.

Mrs. Inkpen cleared her throat, and the students quieted down. She gave them all a pointed look, her eyes briefly lingering on Everin, Phoenix, and Tariel.

"Today's class will be a bit of an introduction to the Language of Dracos. Before we begin, though," she glanced at Jackson, "I'd like to address something unique." She turned to the class with a raised eyebrow. "Jackson here has no record of dragon blood in his family history. Yet, a few days ago, he was able to shapeshift." She paused for dramatic effect. "This is a rare occurrence but not entirely unheard of in the dragon community. Some dragons awaken their abilities later than others, and sometimes, the awakening happens in unexpected ways."

Everin's eyes widened as she turned to Jackson, her mind buzzing with the implications of what Mrs. Inkpen had just revealed. Jackson, who had never shown any signs of being a dragon, had suddenly shapeshifted. She was barely holding back a million questions that she wanted to ask him, but before she could, Mrs. Inkpen continued.

"Jackson, would you like to explain what happened?" she asked, her voice softening.

Jackson shrugged nonchalantly, a faint smile tugging at his lips. "Well, I was just hanging out one day, feeling kind of stressed. All of a sudden, I felt this heat building up in me. Then, boom, dragon form. I couldn't exactly control it, but it happened. It was like... something inside me finally woke up."

"That's incredible," Phoenix murmured, her eyes wide. "I've always known I had it in me, but I can't imagine just getting it like that."

Jackson laughed, clearly still processing the whole experience. "Yeah, trust me, it was a bit of a shock to me too. And then came a man dressed in a suit who claimed to be from the Council of Dragons of the West. He said there are many students like me out here, and to my surprise, I found my best mate, Tariel, here as well."

Mrs. Inkpen nodded thoughtfully. "What happened to Jackson is exactly why we have this class: to help you control your dragon abilities and understand the language of your bloodline. Now, on to today's lesson."

She moved to the front of the room and tapped the smartboard, which flickered to life. The screen displayed the intricate symbols of Dracos, the ancient, flowing language of drag-ons. Each character seemed to pulse with an ancient energy, and Everin felt an odd connection to the letters, as though they resonated with something deep inside her.

"Now," Mrs. Inkpen began, her voice calm but filled with authority. "In our studies, we focus on the basics of Dracos, the written form, its structure, and the core principles behind it. For most of you, since you all carry dragon blood, this will come naturally. With only a little practice, you'll be able to speak and write in Dracos. But first, let's start with the let-ters." She motioned to the smartboard, and the first symbol appeared.

The letters on the screen looked like a blend of sharp, jagged edges and smooth curves, ancient but elegant in their design. Everin leaned forward, fascinated. She had never seen any-thing like it before. The beauty of the language was almost hypnotic.

Mrs. Inkpen whispered a command, and four imposing black boxes rose from her desk, gliding through the air on unseen wings. One settled before each student. Everin's eyes widened at the mystical dark box, its surface etched with an enchanting dragon's claw print.

"Open your Dracos letter box," Mrs. Inkpen instructed, her

voice calm yet filled with anticipation.

Heart pounding, Everin reached out and slowly pulled open the magnetic flap. Inside, swirling black mist gathered into Dracos' letters that seemed to pulse with ancient energy. The letters shifted subtly, alive with magic, yet they never strayed beyond the confines of the box.

"Now, run your fingers over it, oh, hold on, Jackson! Don't actually touch it yet!" Mrs. Inkpen called out, a playful warning in her tone.

She continued, "Channel your inner dragon and try to move those letters with your mind. See if you can make them dance without touching them."

Next to Everin, Tariel was already at work. His hand moved gracefully, and as if by magic, the letters began to follow his every gesture, like an army of tiny ants marching in response to his silent command.

"That's it, Tariel! Keep it up," Mrs. Inkpen praised. "Now, everyone else, focus. Miss Bevington, focus on the letters."

As they began their first lesson on letter recognition, Everin noticed that Tariel was practically fluent. His eyes lit up as he recognized the symbols and whispered the words under his breath, seemingly without effort. Mrs. Inkpen gave him a knowing smile.

"Mr. Fenwick," she said, her voice lifting slightly. "It seems you are well-versed in Dracos already. How about you help the others with the names of the Dracos letters?"

Tariel gave a slight shrug, his casual demeanor intact. "Sure, I can help," he said with a grin. He stood up, walking to the front of the class. "Alright, you guys, let me show you how it's done."

Everin watched him, a mixture of awe and frustration swirling in her chest. It was clear that Tariel had a natural talent for this. He made it seem so easy. She couldn't help but wonder why it didn't come as naturally to her, despite her own dragon blood.

Mrs. Inkpen chuckled softly, sensing the tension in the room. "As I'm sure you're aware," she said, "Tariel and Phoenix both come from families with a long history of dragon shifters, so while they're familiar with the culture, even they're behind on the curriculum. All four of you, Tariel, Phoenix, Jackson, and Everin, have joined partway through the year. That means you'll need to put in extra effort to catch up. We've arranged additional lessons and assignments to help bridge the gap."

Everin felt a pang of anxiety, but she tried to push it aside. She wasn't used to being behind everyone else. She had always been the one whom others wanted to catch up to. But she could tell that this wasn't going to be like her old school. This was different; this was about more than just grades.

As they practiced more, Everin found that the symbols slightly moved with her hand and they didn't feel completely foreign to her. There was something almost instinctive about them, like her mind was starting to connect the dots. But she still felt like she was only scratching the surface. Tariel's fluency only made her more aware of how much ground she had to cover.

She glanced sideways and, quietly, her gaze settled on Jackson. He looked tense, his brow furrowed as he squinted at the same symbols she was beginning to recognize. His lips moved, mouthing silent pronunciations, but it was clear he was struggling to keep up. Everin had always seen Jackson as the golden boy back in school, tall, confident, admired without effort. But here, in the hallowed halls of Drakon Academy, he wasn't the top anymore. At least not in languages. And strangely, that made him feel a little more real to her. A little less untouchable.

By the end of the lesson, Everin was left feeling both accomplished and frustrated. She had learned a lot but still had so much to catch up on. Tariel gave her a reassuring smile before they all headed out of the room.

"Don't worry. The only reason I know Dracos is that I've been studying it with my dad. You know I've always known that as the firstborn, I will shapeshift into a dragon one day," he said softly, walking beside her. "Your case is different. You never knew you were a dragon blood. But you'll get the hang of it. Dracos isn't easy, but it's in our blood. It just takes time."

Everin nodded, though doubts still lingered. Was she really ready for everything that was ahead? She wasn't sure yet, but she knew one thing: she was going to find out.

CHAPTER 9

The Sapphire Shaft

A week later, the training grounds of Drakon stretched wide beneath the morning sun, an open arena ringed by ancient stone walls worn by generations of use. Beyond them, towering trees swayed in the breeze, forming a natural boundary, while the air carried the tang of dust and anticipation. The vast space, where dragons often launched into the skies in practice, now thrummed with sharper energy, as though it sensed something new was about to begin.

Professor Stark, her presence as commanding as ever, gathered the senior students into a loose circle at the edge of the field. Her voice, warm yet threaded with authority, carried clearly across the open space. "Students," she announced, "I'd like you to welcome our new Dragon Combats instructor, Professor Rudiff. He comes to us with a fresh perspective and a calm, steady hand. I trust he will guide you well as you learn to harness your inner dragon."

The man who stepped forward seemed to be in his early

thirties, his dark eyes steady, his posture composed, and there was an unmistakable aura of quiet confidence about him. Professor Rudiff inclined his head slightly in greeting before moving to the center of the arena.

"Good morning, dragons and would-be dragons," he said, his tone calm yet edged with steel. The words seemed to ripple through the air, silencing even the restless shuffling of feet.

Out of the corner of her eye, Everin caught Professor Stark giving a final approving nod before she turned and walked away, her robes trailing behind her as Rudiff took full command of the ground.

He did not waste time. With a sharp sweep of his arm, golden sparks burst from his sleeve, flaring outward until they fanned into the illusion of a vast dragon's wing. The image shimmered brilliantly for a moment, its arc cutting across the air like a blade, before scattering into embers that drifted down and vanished against the dirt. The display was controlled, purposeful, and it held the kind of precision that made the students stand taller, knowing the lesson ahead would demand more than they had ever given before.

Rudiff dropped low, pivoted on one foot, and slid sideways with a crisp sidestep. His boots scraped against the dirt in a clean, practiced rhythm. Straightening again, he said, "That was the Wing Veil Sidestep, which is a basic dragon evasion technique. Simple enough to learn, but executed well, it can mean the difference between a clean escape and taking a claw to the ribs. A dragon uses the full force of its wings to dodge and counter. You," he pointed at the students, "can train the timing and flow right here, in human form."

He dusted his hands as the sparks faded. "Today we focus on combat, flying, evasion, and, yes, attack." He lifted his chin toward the sky. "Those of you who can shift, take to the skies."

Several students transformed on the spot, wings stretching with elegance and power, scales glinting under the sunlight. The air shimmered as Professor Rudiff shifted into his dragon form, a magnificent, navy-blue scaled beast with long, ridged wings and eyes that shimmered like liquid silver. With a powerful leap, he launched into the air and performed a breathtaking aerial maneuver.

While dragons wheeled and turned above, Tariel, Phoenix, and Everin remained on the ground, still waiting for their own dragon forms to awaken.

"Ugh, this is unfair," Phoenix muttered, pulling out her phone to record the dragons mid-flight.

Tariel leaned over her shoulder, then snatched the phone with a smirk. "Get your head out of the phone for once."

"Hey!" she shouted, chasing after him.

Everin giggled. "You know your viewers will just think it's AI-generated. Dragons don't exist, remember?"

Phoenix growled under her breath, quickening her pace to catch Tariel. As she moved, Everin noticed a strange flicker around her, a shimmer of energy rippling at her fingertips, almost like static. Her eyes narrowed. Could Phoenix be closer to shifting than she realized?

Just then, Professor Rudiff descended, landing gracefully. His transformation back into human form was seamless. He stood tall, brushing dirt from his navy robe, a smirk tugging at his lips as he watched the chaos among the late bloomers.

"We'll get there," he said with a glint in his eye. "Some of the most powerful dragons are the ones who take the longest to awaken."

From his leather satchel, he drew out four intricately designed silver shafts, each tipped with a glowing sapphire. He held them high so the late bloomers could see.

"Tariel, Everin, Phoenix," he called. "For you, I have these."

The three hurried back, Phoenix shoving her reclaimed phone into her pocket.

"These are Sapphire Shafts," Rudiff explained, handing one to each of them. "Usually given to first-years before they can fully shapeshift. Students use them until their dragon forms awaken. Most lose track of them once they can transform, but don't underestimate them because these aren't toys."

The late bloomers exchanged nervous glances as they accepted their shafts. Tariel's fingers brushed the cool metal with determination; Everin's heart pounded with both excitement and nervousness; Phoenix eyed hers with a mix of reluctant curiosity and defiant skepticism.

Phoenix turned hers over skeptically. "So… technically every student should have one of these?"

"Yes," Rudiff said firmly. "But this isn't just a training stick. It's a Council weapon, one taught in combat drills to every warrior. Focus your inner power into the shaft and the sapphire will glow. That glow is your first sign of tapping your hidden dragon energy. Master that glow, and you'll be able to channel enough power to strike or even injure a fully formed dragon."

As he spoke, Rudiff placed one hand on the shaft he held.

Slowly, he closed his eyes, and the trio watched as faint streams of light coursed from his palm into the weapon. The intricate designs carved along the silver length began to pulse, one by one, like veins awakening with life. The sapphire at the tip flared to life, shining with a brilliant blue radiance.

"Observe," he said, his voice calm but commanding. He swung the shaft in a smooth arc, and it elongated in his grip with a metallic snap, stretching into a weapon taller than he was. With another twist of his wrist, the shaft contracted, folding neatly back to a shorter size, light still dancing across its surface.

Then, with a firm stance, Rudiff raised the weapon overhead. A surge of energy rippled outward as he brought it down in a controlled strike. The sapphire released a concentrated wave of blue force that cracked against the stone floor, leaving a faint scorch mark that shimmered with residual sparks.

"This," he explained, lowering the shaft, "is how you connect with it. The weapon amplifies your energy, but it requires focus and discipline. Without control, it is only silver and stone. With mastery, it becomes an extension of your dragon self."

He held the shaft out toward the trio, the glow fading slowly as if the weapon were breathing.

"Now, I want you to head to the practice zone," Professor Rudiff instructed, pointing to a sheltered area framed by an ancient stone arch. "Direct your energy toward the shaft and focus on making the sapphire glow. This is the first step in learning to defend yourselves against the might of a full dragon's claws and breath."

Several minutes later, as the fully transformed students, including Jackson, soared overhead in magnificent dragon forms, engaging in exhilarating aerial duels, a few onlookers couldn't resist teasing the late bloomers.

"Hey, check out the newbies with their magic sticks!" one student jeered, laughter echoing across the field.

"Maybe those sticks will do better than your half-hearted shifts!" another chimed in, drawing snickers from a small group of peers.

Tariel clenched his jaw and exchanged a determined look with Everin. "Let's show them we're not just here for decoration," he murmured.

Retreating to their practice zone, Tariel and Everin focused intently on their shafts. With closed eyes and steady breaths, they channeled the untapped energy simmering within them. Everin reached out tentatively and, after a moment of silence, felt a slight pulse from the sapphire as it began to emit a faint, pulsing glow. It was small, barely more than a shimmer, but it was progress.

"Did you see that?" Tariel whispered, excitement bubbling in his voice as he mimicked her gesture. His own shaft's sapphire flickered in response, a modest yet encouraging sign.

Encouraged, Everin tried again. She moved her hand in slow, deliberate motions, channeling her inner strength. The sapphire's glow grew a fraction brighter, though it still paled in comparison to the dazzling displays of their fully transformed peers.

Across the sheltered field, Phoenix struggled with her own shaft. Despite several attempts, its sapphire remained stubbornly dim. A few passing students snickered, whispering, "Maybe she's all talk and no spark," which only deepened her frown.

Professor Rudiff strolled over, his calm demeanor cutting through the teasing murmurs. "Remember, mastery takes time," he advised gently. "Focus on feeling the energy inside you. Don't force it. Let it flow naturally to the shaft, and trust that it will respond in its own time."

Tariel and Everin exchanged determined looks as they resumed their practice. Every so often, their fingers brushed against the shaft, and every so often, the sapphire pulsed with a delicate light, a small victory on the path to mastery.

After what felt like an eternity of concentration, Tariel managed to coax the sapphire into a steady, soft glow. Everin's shaft began to pulse rhythmically as well, though its light was still modest. Panting and sweating, Tariel remarked, "We did it… sort of. But look, Everin, our shafts are still weak. Imagine facing a full dragon with claws that could tear through stone or breath that could melt metal."

Everin nodded, worry mingling with resolve. "I know. It's like we're only scratching the surface. We have a long way to go before we can really defend ourselves."

Professor Rudiff returned, his gaze sweeping over the group with a nod of approval. "Every spark of light is a victory," he said softly. "Today, you've taken the first step in unlocking your true potential. Keep practicing, and soon you will harness the power necessary to stand against even the mightiest dragons."

As the session drew to a close, the sounds of battle, roaring transformations, and the occasional triumphant cry filled the air. Though Tariel, Everin, and Phoenix knew their journey was only beginning, they vowed silently to rise to the challenge. With the new guidance of Professor Rudiff, and the steady introduction by Professor Stark, they would not be left behind. Their inner dragons would soon ignite, and one day, their shafts would shine as brilliantly as the legends they were destined to become.

CHAPTER 10

The Trial of Flame and Focus

A few weeks passed, and life at Drakon Academy began to settle into a strange rhythm for Everin. Though she still hadn't fully transformed, her days were filled with lessons, drills, and whispers of prophecy that she pretended not to hear. What surprised her most was that the Academy was starting to feel almost... normal.

In Professor Rudiff's combat class, Everin found herself improving. The sapphire shaft, the enchanted staff used for training, had grown less foreign in her hands. It responded more to her instincts now, humming softly when she gripped it tightly, glowing when her emotions flared. She still didn't quite understand the connection, but she felt it building.

On a breezy afternoon in the combat arena, Professor Rudiff stood before them, his arms crossed, eyes scanning the crowd. The open field buzzed with anticipation. The scent of scorched grass and smoke lingered from earlier drills.

"Today, we're doing a trial combat round," he announced, his deep voice echoing off the arena walls. "I want to see how our late bloomers are adapting to battle scenarios."

A groan came from somewhere in the crowd.

"He wants to fry us today," muttered Garry Goldwin, the chubby teen who had already sweat through his T-shirt, clutching his shaft like a lifeline.

"Rhodes, James, and Jackson, you'll be dragons today."

The three boys transformed with ease. Rhodes was a sleek silver dragon with narrow wings and sharp yellow eyes. James became a hulking bronze creature, his flames sputtering like wild fireworks. Jackson, well, he was a slightly-too-large green dragon who still couldn't land without wobbling like a shopping cart with a bad wheel.

From the stands, Tariya snorted. "Jackson's trying to flap like he's doing Zumba."

"Still can't fly straight," Everin murmured, trying not to laugh. She still couldn't believe that this was the same tall, perfect hunk she'd admired in school.

Tariel grinned. "He tries his best."

Professor Rudiff called out again. "Tariel, Phoenix, and Everin. You three are on defense. Sapphire shafts only. I want coordination, not chaos. Let's see what late bloomers can do."

They entered the arena, shafts ready. The dragon-boys circled above.

Everin tightened her grip on her shaft, the cool metal humming faintly in her hands. As confident as she was growing in her training, a chill worked its way down her spine. These were their classmates, transformed into dragons, yes, but still controlled and contained. What if she ever had to face a real dragon? One wild with fury, flame, and killing intent?

Could a sapphire shaft really protect her from that?

The thought made her heart pound a little harder, but she shook it off. Not now. She had a battle to fight.

Ameera Morgraff, the nerdy girl with big glasses and a bigger attitude, whispered to Tariya from the benches, "This is either going to be history or a flaming disaster."

"On my mark," Rudiff called. "Begin!"

With a thunderous cry, James swooped down, fire spewing from his jaws. Phoenix rolled behind a boulder. Tariel leapt forward and deflected with his shaft. Everin ducked, then spun to strike at Jackson's approaching wing.

Her shaft sparked against his scales, and with a yelp, Jackson spiraled to the ground, transforming back into his human form mid-fall and landing on his butt with a groan.

"That's one!" Tariel shouted.

Rhodes and James doubled back. Phoenix emerged, holding her shaft like a blade. "Coming left!"

Everin and Tariel moved instinctively, forming a triangle. Flames shot toward them, and they raised their shafts in defense. The enchanted metal glowed.

Phoenix channeled something deeper this time. Her shaft pulsed with energy and launched forward, hitting Rhodes squarely in the chest. He tumbled through the air, roaring in surprise as he slammed into a rock face and slid down in human form.

The crowd cheered. Tariya whistled loudly, startling Garry, who dropped his notes.

But James wasn't done. The bronze dragon reared back and launched a full column of fire at them.

"Together!" Tariel yelled.

Everin, Phoenix, and Tariel planted their feet, raised their shafts, and focused. As James's flames reached them, the shafts interlocked, forming a shimmering barrier of light.

The arena gasped. Fire blazed against the barrier—and held. A ripple of blue light shimmered outward, redirecting the flames sharply to the right, where it narrowly missed a group of students, including Garry and Ameera.

"Whoa! Watch the fire fountain!" Garry yelped, diving behind a bench.

Ameera huffed, adjusting her scarf. "Next time, warn us before you unleash your inner dragon."

James broke off, stunned. He hovered, then slowly descended and changed back, eyes wide.

Professor Rudiff strode forward, a rare grin tugging at his lips. "Impressive. The resonance of combined late-bloomer energy. That's not something you see every day."

Phoenix was panting, her face flushed with pride. Everin blinked in disbelief.

"Did we really just... do that?" she asked.

Tariel bumped her shoulder gently. "Looks like we did."

Cheers erupted from the watching students. For the first time since arriving, Everin didn't feel behind.

She felt powerful.

And more than anything, she knew now: They were only just getting started.

Just then, a shimmering dragon scale came whooshing through the sky, spinning like a disc of light and heat. It hovered briefly before zipping toward Professor Rudiff's outstretched hand. He caught it smoothly and held it up.

With a swipe of his clawed hand over the scale's surface, a glimmer of dragon energy surged through it. A golden shimmer erupted in the air, and a glowing audio projection crackled to life.

It was the voice of Headmaster Fenwick.

"All students are to report to the Grand Assembly Hall immediately. This is a formal summons by the Dragon Council of the West. Attendance is mandatory."

A collective murmur ran through the crowd. The Grand Assembly Hall was rarely used except for major events.

Professor Rudiff's brow furrowed. "Everyone, move in an orderly fashion. Now."

"Why so sudden?" a student asked aloud.

"What's going on?" whispered another.

Even Professor Rudiff looked puzzled. "I don't know," he said. "But we're about to find out."

CHAPTER 11

The Announcement

The Grand Assembly Hall, an enormous dome-shaped chamber of shimmering obsidian and silver-veined columns, buzzed with the footsteps and hushed murmurs of hundreds of students. Ornate dragon carvings lined the walls, their eyes seeming to watch every movement. Above, ethereal chandeliers made of floating crystal shards illuminated the space with soft amber light.

Everin took her seat near the middle rows alongside Tariel, Phoenix, and Jackson. All of them looked curious, even slightly anxious. The air carried an undeniable tension, like the sky before a storm.

At the front of the hall, the high platform was flanked by two flame-wreathed dragon statues, and from behind them stepped Chief Professor Fenwick, Headmaster of Drakon Academy. His deep voice echoed as he stood behind a podium fashioned from a massive dragon scale, gleaming with enchantment.

"Students of Drakon Academy," he began, "thank you for assembling on such short notice. I won't delay you long, but what I have to announce is of great importance. Today, we are honored by the presence of Chief Mariah Mac Naught, Head of the Western Dragon Council."

A collective ripple of excitement passed through the crowd. Heads turned as a tall, commanding figure with a dark navy cloak and shimmering silver-streaked hair stepped onto the stage. Her piercing eyes, so sharp they felt like they could slice through bone, scanned the assembly. She moved with elegance and danger, like fire given shape.

Everin shifted in her seat. Something about the woman felt heavier than her presence. Like gravity itself bent toward her.

Mariah placed her hand on the scale podium. The scale responded, glowing slightly, amplifying her voice with a smooth, magical resonance.

"Thank you, Headmaster Fenwick," she said, her tone both regal and razor-sharp. "Every year, during the final term, we host a longstanding tradition, the Dragon of the Year Competition. A contest of skill, strength, magic, and leadership, open only to our final year students."

The final years leaned forward slightly, some smirking, others whispering.

"But this year," Mariah continued, "the Dragon Council has decided to make a rare exception. Final year students, ages seventeen and eighteen, will be allowed to enter as always, and for the first time, sixteen-year-olds from the senior class may also take part."

A stunned silence followed.

Everin looked up toward the elevated seating where the final years sat and saw their brows furrow. A few looked outright insulted.

Mariah wasn't finished. "Additionally, the timing of the competition has changed. It will no longer be held in Term Four. This year, it will occur three weeks from today, at the end of Term Three."

That did it. A low, confused rumble spread through the room. Whispers became chatter.

"Three weeks?" Jackson whispered behind Everin. "Is that even enough time to prepare?"

Everin looked toward the stage again. For a brief second,

she caught Mariah's eyes and felt a flicker of something she couldn't name. Like the Chief wasn't just looking at her, but through her. Measuring her.

The moment ended as the assembly was dismissed. Students rose from their seats in waves, filing out through the carved archways, their conversations animated.

"This isn't fair," grumbled a striking Finals student with silver hair streaked in pink. Everin heard someone whisper his name, Zale Nightwind, as he passed. "Why are they even letting under shifters in?"

"Must be desperate for talent," an equally handsome boy walking beside Zale sneered.

James, in full teasing form, elbowed Tariel as they exited. "Guess that rules you out, Fenwick. You and your late-bloomer girlfriend, what are you gonna do? Sparkle at them with your shafts?"

Everin flushed. "We're not—"

"Relax," Tariel muttered with a grin. "He's just scared I'll win in style."

Phoenix and Tariya caught up to them, weaving through the

crowd.

"Well, now you understand what I meant," Phoenix said, clearly annoyed. "The Council's watching us like test subjects. First the summons, now this."

Tariel nodded, face serious. "Feels like they're pushing us to shapeshift. Forcing it, even."

Everin exhaled slowly. "But why? Why now?"

No one answered. But in her gut, Everin knew the timing wasn't a coincidence. The Council wanted something.

And she was sure of one thing: the countdown had begun.

Tariel lingered as Everin disappeared with Phoenix and Tariya toward the girls' dorm. Jackson fell in step beside him, hands shoved in his pockets.

"Three weeks," Jackson muttered, shaking his head. "A bit harsh, don't you think? Feels like the Council's trying to squeeze us. No room for late bloomers anymore. They want answers, and fast."

"Maybe," Tariel said lightly, forcing a half-grin. "Or maybe they just like watching us sweat."

Jackson snorted. "You joke, but they are not playing around. They want everyone shifting, no excuses." He clapped Tariel on the shoulder before heading toward the boys' dormitory. "Better get ready. This is not going to be pretty."

Tariel watched him go, his grin fading. He stood in the courtyard for a long moment, then turned and walked toward the meditation chamber.

He had been coming here for weeks, hoping the stillness would unlock something inside him. So far, nothing had changed.

The chamber was carved deep into the stone of the Academy, dimly lit by rows of flickering candles. The walls were etched with intricate designs, stories of dragons long past, etched so finely they seemed alive when the candlelight touched them. Shimmering enchantments lingered in the air, a faint aura that promised peace and clarity to those who entered.

Long white curtains hung at the far end, stirring with a wind that had no clear source. It carried a low hum, the sound of air moving through the hidden veins of the mountain. The place felt alive, steeped in centuries of prayer and striving.

Tariel sank cross-legged to the floor, resting his palms on his knees. He drew in a breath, then another. He visualized wings, fire, the raw power of shifting. Nothing came. His jaw tightened. He tried again, focusing harder, until the world around him seemed to fade.

And then he saw it.

Behind his closed eyes, something stirred. Not light, not calm, but a vast abyss, glowing with a red, fiery pulse. It drew him closer, as though the ground beneath his mind tilted toward its edge. The flames shifted like shadows alive, flickering shapes just beyond his reach. The air in his lungs burned, his chest tightening as though the abyss itself was pressing into him.

During the vision, his thoughts rose like those of a lucid dreamer. His thoughts fluttered. *This must be a glimpse of hell. Freaking hell. Even in a meditation chamber, I still can't focus my dragon energy properly.*

His eyes snapped open, breath ragged, sweat running down his temple. The candles still flickered, the curtains still stirred. Yet the image clung to him, heavy and searing, like a secret he had no right to glimpse.

He pressed his hands against the stone floor. "I have to do

this," he whispered to the empty chamber. "I have to shift. No more excuses."

He grabbed a book from a nearby shelf, flipping through diagrams of posture, breathing, and energy channels. He tried them all until his muscles trembled, muttered half-remembered incantations under his breath, and stretched until his back ached. Nothing.

"Come on," he groaned, lying flat on the floor, arms spread wide. "Anytime now. Feel free to unleash the mighty dragon." The silence that answered made him grit his teeth.

Still, he sat up again, determination burning through the exhaustion. He would not stay trapped in the Seniors forever. He would not be remembered as the boy who never shifted. Late bloomer or not, he would prove himself.

"I will win," he vowed into the still air. "I will show them all."

The curtains stirred, carrying that strange, sourceless wind, and for a heartbeat, Tariel swore the chamber was listening.

Later that evening, in their shared dorm room, Phoenix threw her iPad onto the bed, nearly bouncing it off the mattress. "Did you two know," she said, eyes gleaming, "that the Seniors who qualify for the final rounds will be invited to the celebration party after the competition?"

Everin looked up, surprised. "Wait, I thought that was only for final-year students."

"Normally, yes!" Phoenix said, bouncing a little on her heels. "But this year's announcement says Seniors who reach the finals can go too."

Tariya raised a skeptical eyebrow and snatched her phone from the nightstand. "I'm going to need to see that for myself."

After a few taps, she frowned. "She's not wrong. But I wouldn't get too excited. You have to survive the qualifying rounds first."

Everin sighed, flopping back on her bed. "Not that it matters to me. I haven't even shapeshifted yet."

"Oh, come on," Phoenix said, already imagining gowns and glitter. "Party! Do you know who's going to be there? Thorian Ashmore and Zale Nightwind. Absolute stunners. Both are from top dragon clans. One of them is definitely going to win. Probably Thorian, he's insane in duels."

Everin blinked. "Those two? Weren't they the ones scowling like someone ruined their dinner during the announcement?"

"Exactly," Phoenix said, smirking. "They weren't thrilled about sharing the spotlight. But maybe they'll come to terms with it. Especially once they see my dress."

Tariya rolled her eyes. "Someone's already planning the playlist."

Everin noticed the way Phoenix's excitement burned brighter with every word, how badly she wanted the spotlight, the party, the chance to shine in front of Thorian and Zale. That was her fuel. Everin's was different. She wasn't dreaming about limelight or dresses. She wanted to stand in that arena, wings unfurled, showing everyone, including the Council, that she wasn't weak. That being a miner's daughter didn't make her less. That being late to shift didn't make her broken.

She wanted to prove she belonged not just to her classmates, or to the Council, but to herself. Three weeks wasn't long. And as she stared at the ceiling, her pulse quickening, one truth pressed into her heart like fire waiting to break free.

The countdown to the competition had begun, and Everin was determined to do anything in her power to shapeshift.

CHAPTER 12

Sparks and Scales

The late morning sun filtered through the wide hexagonal skylights of the Shapeshifting Arena, casting golden beams onto the marble floor below. The space echoed with the sound of grunts, magical energy, and frustration. Today was no ordinary training session; it was the shapeshifting class with Professor Stark, and the pressure was higher than ever.

"Focus! Channel the heat, the intent. You are dragons, not dithering pigeons!" barked Professor Stark, pacing with the fire of a general before battle. Her crimson robes trailed behind her, sparking slightly with static as she moved.

Everin maintained composure as she made another attempt, standing within her assigned glyph circle, hands extended and breathing evenly. Nothing. No flame. No shimmer of scales. Just warmth in her chest, pulsing but elusive.

Across the arena, Phoenix grit her teeth and inhaled deeply. Her fingers curled, her spine arched, and for a heartbeat, her outline flickered, traced in glimmering faint shimmer of heat.

Then it vanished.

A few students gasped. One in the back muttered, "Did you see that? Bevington blood, definitely."

Phoenix staggered back a step, breath catching in her throat, but instead of pushing herself to try again, she scoffed and pulled her phone from her sleeve pocket. With a theatrical flick, she tilted the camera toward herself. "And here we are, live from Drakon Academy," she said loudly, her tone sweet as venom. "Some of us are working hard to spark, while others are just perfecting their glare." She cast a pointed glance at Professor Stark.

The students around her tittered, a ripple of laughter breaking through the tension.

Then a surge of dragon energy cracked the air. Phoenix yelped as her phone ripped from her hand and snapped neatly into Stark's waiting palm.

"Hey! My phone!" Phoenix shouted, staring in disbelief at her empty fingers.

Stark's voice cut through the laughter. "You spark for half a second, then make a mockery of the training ground? Enough. You will spend the rest of the day in the Meditation Chamber."

Phoenix tossed her hair back with a sharp scoff. "Fine. I'll go to the Meditation Chamber. But can I have my phone back now?"

"No." Stark's eyes narrowed, her tone steely. "You'll collect it after your session is complete this afternoon. And, as per academy rules, when a student's device is confiscated, their parents are informed."

That struck the nerve.

Phoenix's bravado cracked. Her voice rose, sharp and raw, shaking with anger. "Parents informed? Do you really think my father cares whether I shift or not? He doesn't care! No one in my family does. I don't need to be a dragon to serve any-one. I'll always be a Bevington. I'll always be rich. And I don't see the point of any of this!" Her voice trembled now, slip-ping between fury and hurt. "For once, why can't people just let me be who I want to be? I don't want this. I don't want to end up like those dragons who sign a century-long contract at Dragon's Bricks or the mines. Smelting ores until their scales peel, trapped in servitude with no life of their own. That is not going to be me."

Silence fell across the training ground, heavy and absolute.

Everin's chest tightened. Dragon's Bricks. Century-long contracts. Was that why her father never came home? The thought coiled in her mind like smoke, dark and unwelcome. A hundred years… by the time he returned, his family would be gone. Was that the reason for his distance all along?

Professor Stark's expression didn't change. She only gestured firmly toward the gates. "Meditation chamber. Now."

Phoenix spun on her heel, braid lashing behind her like a whip, but this time there was no laughter from the students. Only the echo of her words hanging heavy in the air.

As she passed Everin and Tariel, a faint outline of fire coiled around her form again, an echo of wings and flame, but it fizzled before anyone could say a word.

Jackson leaned toward Tariel and Everin, his voice low. "Is she okay? That wasn't normal."

Tariel shrugged. "She's close. Whatever's inside her is starting to wake up."

Everin bit her lip. She could feel it too; Phoenix was brimming with energy, like a volcano capped too tight.

Near the front, Professor Stark turned to the rest of the class. "A reminder," she said sharply, "The Dragon of the Year Competition is only three weeks away. Shapeshifting must be smooth and complete, no half-transforms, no wobbly feet, no flailing wings. The Council expects precision. If you haven't shifted by then, you won't qualify."

Her gaze swept the class, then locked pointedly onto Everin, Tariel, and Jackson. "No exceptions. Late bloomers or not."

Groans and murmurs passed through the class. Everin's stomach twisted.

Just then, Tariya Gratton finished her glyph sequence with a confident spin. Her body shimmered, limbs elongating briefly before she pulled them back with expert control. A glint of scales ran up her arms and shoulders before changing into a flawless, contained shift.

"Excellent control, Tariya," Stark nodded. "That's how you command the transformation. Not with tantrums."

Tariya smiled modestly, brushing a curly strand behind her

ear. Jackson, standing nearby, whispered to Everin with a grin, "I think Tariya's wearing one of those shapeshifter suits... you know, the Aegisweave ones. Smart move. If I shifted now, I'd probably combust my pants off."

Just then, a faint sizzling sound and a thin wisp of smoke curled from the hem of Jackson's trousers. He yelped, leaping a step back.

Tariel raised an eyebrow. "Did you actually try to shift without Aegisweave?"

Jackson grimaced. "Just a tiny test! I thought I had control. Apparently, my pants disagree."

Everin snorted. "Please don't." She had always imagined Jackson as that ultimate god who would never make any mistake, but here she was witnessing that the basketball team's captain was setting his pants on fire.

Tariel added dryly, "I'm sure that's how legends are made." Jackson winked. "Hey, some of us are here to make an impression."

Laughter rippled between them, easing the pressure for just a moment. But beneath the jokes, Everin felt the clock ticking in her bones. Three weeks until the competition.

Three weeks to figure out who, or what, she really was.

Later that afternoon, the golden light slanted through the soaring windows of the Dragon's Abode of Literature. The scent of old parchment, dust, and flickering magical wards drifted through the air. Everin stood beside Tariya at one of the long wooden tables, a pile of books on ancient transformation glyphs scattered before them. Overhead, smaller dragons flitted through the rafters, delivering scrolls and tomes with practiced ease.

Everin huffed, flipping through another book. "There's nothing in here about how to transform faster. Just the usual breathwork and elemental syncing."

Tariya didn't look up. "That's because you're not looking in the right section."

"Is there a right section?" Everin asked, raising an eyebrow.

"Restricted section," came a familiar voice behind them.

Everin turned, and there was Tariel, leaning against the end of the table, his usual lopsided smile in place. The afternoon light framed his face in a golden glow, and his green eyes sparkled with mischief. Her breath hitched, just slightly, and her stomach gave an odd flutter.

He held up a small, rune-etched key. "I might know a way in."

CHAPTER 13

The Forbidden Catalyst

The library was quieter than usual that morning, a faint glow of filtered sunlight slanting through the high glass arches. Everin trailed behind Tariel and Tariya as they moved purposefully toward the far northern wall. This part of the Dragon's Abode of Literature was almost deserted, save for the occasional flutter of parchment wings as a dragon courier zipped past overhead.

Everin's boots clicked softly on the stone floor as they approached a shadowed, rocky stretch of wall carved with what looked like hundreds of intricate dragon sculptures. Each was unique, some fierce, others serene, and nestled between them were rows of ancient lanterns, some still glowing with soft enchanted fire. The place felt like stepping into the belly of a dragon temple.

"Whoa," Everin whispered, unable to stop herself. "Okay, this is... cooler than cool."

Tariel grinned and approached a line of lanterns shaped like small, dull ovals. "This is where it gets interesting," he said, his voice low. "There's a pattern to these. Each lamp represents a color in the spectrum."

He began turning the lamps, one by one, clockwise, starting with Ryvellen, Orenth, and Gildor, murmuring a tune under his breath.

"Are you... singing?" Tariya raised an eyebrow.

"It helps me remember the order," Tariel replied, not missing a beat. "Ryvellen-Orenth-Gildor-Bravain-Irieth-Volarin, it's an ancient dragon mnemonic. Each name corresponds to a hue in the Prism Flame Spectrum."

As he reached the final lamp, Volarin, he gave it a slow, deliberate turn.

Everin leaned in and whispered, "If this opens a portal to a dragon karaoke lounge, I'm leaving."

With a soft groan and the rumble of hidden gears, the stone wall split down the center. A narrow doorway appeared where moments ago there had been only rock and sculpture.

Everin blinked. "Okay, not a karaoke lounge. Slightly disappointed."

The trio stepped into the passage beyond. As soon as their feet crossed the threshold, dim crystals embedded in the floor lit up one by one, revealing a descending path. Ahead stood another door, this one made of dark ironwood etched with dragons in flight and a central golden lock shaped like a flaming eye.

"Got this from my dad," Tariel murmured, pulling out a small brass key. "While he was asleep. Technically, he won't miss it."

Everin gave him a sidelong look. "Technically, you're a thief."

"Technically," he agreed, slipping the key into the lock. The door clicked open.

The Restricted Section of the Dragon's Abode of Literature felt heavier than the rest of the library, the air cooler, the silence sharper, as if the shelves themselves disapproved of being disturbed. Everin followed close behind Tariel and Tariya, her breath caught in her throat, every step measured as they slipped deeper between the looming bookcases. The smell of dust and ink clung to the air, the faint flicker of enchanted lanterns throwing long shadows across the floor.

Then she froze. Ahead of them, moving along one of the tables stacked with books, was Professor Stark. Her arms were filled with heavy volumes pressed tight against her side as she muttered irritably under her breath. The three of them exchanged quick, tense glances before slipping into the shadows of the tall shelves, pressing themselves against the carved pillars between the rows, half-hidden but still upright, their bodies stiff with the effort of being unseen.

Stark dropped the books on the long wooden table with a thud that seemed to echo through the entire chamber. She opened one, her lips pursed as her eyes scanned the glowing title. Everin could just make it out between the gaps in the shelves. *Draconic Awakening Elixirs.*

Her heart thudded. Was Stark researching? The thought darted through her mind with a sting. Did she know more than she let on?

A faint rustle, maybe the shift of their shadows, seemed to catch Stark's notice. She straightened from the table and began to move.

The scrape of Stark's shoes shifted closer. Her head turned slowly toward the shelves, her eyes sweeping the dim rows where Everin and the others held their breath.

Tariya slipped into the next aisle, her footsteps soft as shadows.

Everin pressed tighter against the shelf. Her shoulder brushed a stack of heavy books and the cool curve of an ornate vase wedged between them. Its surface was etched with overlapping dragon scales, the faint outline of eyes carved into the clay.

Her fingers brushed it.

The vase shuddered. The scaled ridges warmed beneath her touch, and the eyes snapped open. Molten red light flared in the dimness, casting sharp shadows across the shelves. A guttural rumble rolled from its hollow belly, like a dragon warning intruders away.

Everin's breath caught. Panic surged. She parted her lips to scream.

Tariel moved first. His hand cut through the air in a swift arc. Sparks leapt from his fingertips.

The glow in the vase flickered, then went dark. The rumble cut off. The carved eyes dulled back into lifeless stone.

In the same heartbeat, his arm closed around her. He pulled

her back against him, his palm covering her mouth. Her spine pressed into the solid thrum of his chest, his heartbeat pounding through her.

She froze. Every nerve screamed awake. The sharp scent of pine and cedar clung to him, flooding her senses. His breath brushed her ear, low and steady.

"Shush."

Her pulse raced wildly, louder than her thoughts, louder than Stark's footsteps that moved closer, paused, then drifted away again. She remained still in his hold, her heart fluttering against his palm, and for a fleeting, terrifying moment, she wasn't sure if it was fear or something else making her knees weak.

Professor Stark stopped at the table, snapped a book shut with sharp disapproval, and muttered to herself. "Elixirs, transformations, forbidden techniques. Half of it never worked." She flicked her wrist sharply.

Two draggrels shuffled from the shadows, their stone-gray forms bent and grumbling. She thrust the books at them. "Put these away properly. And stop lazing about in here, this place is a disgrace."

The draggrels muttered as they obeyed. One, slower than the other, grumbled in its gravelly voice as it stacked the pile. "Not useless. Not ancient either. Still works. Still helps humans to shapeshift into dragons faster."

Everin's eyes widened, her breath hot against Tariel's hand. She glanced up at him, but his gaze stayed fixed on Stark.

At last, Stark gathered her armful of books and swept away, her footsteps fading into silence. The draggrels lumbered after her, leaving only the lingering echo of their complaints.

Tariel's hand slowly slipped from Everin's mouth, though he did not step back, and she could still feel the warmth of his chest against her back. She lowered her gaze quickly, afraid he would notice the flush burning in her cheeks.

Tariya reappeared from the aisle, nodding toward the table.

The three of them hurried forward, seizing the book the draggrel had left behind. The letters shimmered faintly, glowing with enchantment. *Igniflorum Primus.*

They read quickly, the words pulling them in. Emberroot, blooming in fire-churned soil beneath a full moon. Veilvine sap, taken from the cliffs of Aether Gorge. Scale dust, drawn from a living Alpha dragon.

Everin's stomach knotted tighter with every line. "This is impossible," she whispered. "I don't even know what these things are, or where to find them. It's beyond us."

Tariel's voice was steady, firm, almost stubborn. "We won't know unless we try. We can research. We can figure it out."

Tariya pulled out her phone and snapped quick photos of the pages, her sharp eyes flicking back and forth. "At least we'll have the recipe later, if we manage to get the ingredients."

Everin brushed her fingers over the glowing script, her chest heavy, her thoughts tangled between fear and possibility.

They closed the book and slipped it back into the shadows of the shelf.

And then Everin felt it. A shift in the air behind them. She turned her head just in time to catch a flicker of movement at the end of the aisle. A shadow slid quickly past, vanishing into the deeper dark.

Her chest tightened. For a heartbeat, she thought she recognized the cut of a shoulder, the tilt of a head, but it was gone too quickly to be sure.

Her skin prickled. Someone had been watching.

That evening, the dining hall buzzed with the low hum of conversation and clinking cutlery. The scent of roasted meats, fresh bread, and enchanted spice drifted through the air.

In one quieter corner of the long, fire-lit chamber, Tariel, Tariya, Everin, and Jackson sat around a carved obsidian table. Trays of food were scattered between them, but conversation was hushed.

At a nearby table sat the infamous Finals group with the two popular leaders, Thorian Ashmore and Zale Nightwind. The boys were loud and confident, their casual jackets accented by gleaming pins etched with the sigils of elite dragon families.

"Did you hear?" Thorian's voice boomed. "Some Seniors still haven't shifted. What are they doing here? Shouldn't they be in the junior wings?"

Zale chuckled. "Maybe they're here to learn embroidery. Certainly not dragon combat."

Ryven smirked and sipped from a goblet. "This competition's going to be easy. Let the flame-flickers stay out of our way."

Just then, Phoenix walked in, her golden braid slightly messy from a long day in the Meditation Chamber. Her face was drawn with fatigue as she slumped on a seat next to Jackson, until she spotted the final years. In a blink, she straightened, smoothed her braid, and dabbed her eyes with a napkin.

Jackson, being polite, scooped a ladle of stew onto her bowl. "Long day?" he asked, glancing sympathetically.

Phoenix took a spoonful of the food without looking. "Mm-hmm," she murmured, her eyes still locked on the final years.

Tariya rolled her eyes. "Honestly, he's not even that tall."

Everin snorted. "Which one?"

Tariya flicked her fingers dismissively. "All of them."

She then tapped into her tablet, scrolling through the Academy's official site, called the DrakoriaNet. "By the way, a field trip has been listed for Saturday, two weeks from today. We get clearance to visit Ashmomere, a small town located below the cliffs. Shopping, potion supplies, baked goods, and whatever you fancy."

Everin perked up. "We're allowed to leave campus?"

"Once every four weeks," Tariya confirmed. "Only with permits. But it's supervised."

Tariel leaned closer over his plate, his voice low. "Which means it's our chance. The elixir ingredients. If we want them, that's when we get them."

Everin shook her head quickly. "No. That's too risky. We'll get caught."

Phoenix smirked, stabbing a strawberry with her fork. "Risky, sure. But worth it. You really think we'll shift in time without help?"

Silence settled over the table. Everin's chest tightened as she looked from one face to the next. One by one, they nodded. Even Tariya, usually cautious, didn't object.

Everin's pulse quickened. She felt the weight of it settle between them like a secret.

Saturday couldn't come soon enough.

CHAPTER 14

The Elixir Plan

The girls' dorm room was dark, but not quiet.

Phoenix let out a dramatic sigh and sat up in her bed, her phone flashlight glowing beneath the sheets. "Are we seriously doing this? Hunting down ancient plants and stirring up magical potions? What if we mess it up and explode? Or worse, get pimples on our face?"

Across the room, Everin switched on her bedside lamp and sat up, clutching a few photocopied parchment sheets. "Too late. I already scanned the recipe."

Tariya sat up too, squinting. "You printed it?"

Everin grinned, waving the translated pages. "Thanks to your scanner charm, it's now in English. It wasn't easy because half of it was smudged with what I hope was ink."

The three girls gathered on Everin's bed, the glow of the lamp casting soft shadows across their faces. Tariya tapped the page, reading aloud.

"Feathered Emberroot. Blooms only under a full moon in fire-churned soil."

Phoenix blinked. "Wait… isn't the full moon this Saturday?"

Tariya nodded. "It is. And—this just updated on the Academy's DrakoriaNet site." She flicked her phone toward them. "Ashmomere's field trip has been moved up. We're going this weekend instead of next."

Everin frowned. "Why?"

"There's a special invitation from the Mayor of Ashmomere," Tariya explained, scrolling. "Apparently, there's a local celebration this Saturday night. A community event which the locals call the Moonlight Revels. There'll be dancing, food, and different kinds of contests."

Phoenix perked up. "Fashion? Dance? Please let it be a make-up competition."

Tariya raised an eyebrow. "You're hopeless."

"Hopelessly stylish," Phoenix corrected. "So we go to the

town, sneak off when no one's looking, grab the root, and boom, the first ingredient will be done."

Everin bit her lip. "Except we don't even know where to look."

Tariya flipped to the back of the recipe notes. "Here. According to this old grimoire, there's a patch of fire-churned soil just outside Ashmomere, that is, near the volcanic ridge. Scarred land from magical flare-ups years ago."

Everin blinked. "So the location's real?"

Tariya nodded. "Yup. But the catch is, Emberroot only blooms for a few hours under the full moon. If we miss it…"

"We wait a whole month," Everin finished.

Phoenix flopped backward on the bed with a groan. "Of course. Nothing about this elixir is easy."

Everin looked down at the next ingredient.

"Veilvine Sap…" she read. "No clue what that is."

Tariya leaned closer. "We'll figure that out after we get the root. One quest at a time."

Phoenix raised her phone again. "And just to confirm—this is totally normal, right? Skipping school rules, wandering out at midnight to find magical plant roots…?"

Everin smirked. "At Drakon Academy? Feels about right."

Just then, Everin's phone buzzed. She glanced at the screen—it was Tariel. When she answered, to her surprise, she heard not one but two voices on the line.

"Hello?" Everin said, blinking.

"Hey, Haydon," Tariel's smooth voice came through, calm and confident. "Jackson and I are calling from my dad's quarters."

Everin arched a brow. "I thought you stayed in the boys' dormitory."

"We do," Tariel replied. "Different wings. But since we needed to talk about the elixir plan, I asked my dad if Jackson could stay the night. Figured it'd be easier to plan if we're in the same room."

Everin felt an odd flutter in her chest. Something about hearing Tariel's voice on the phone felt closer, more casual, and it sent a strange warmth blooming under her ribs. She tried to focus, even as his voice echoed in her ears.

From the other end, Jackson's voice chimed in, "We've been combing through those old potion books. I still can't believe this is real."

"Believe it," Tariel said. "And we're getting that root Saturday night. Are you three ready?"

Phoenix leaned closer to Everin's phone. "Ready? I was born ready."

Tariya snorted. "You were born with glitter and hair serum, more like."

Everin laughed, still staring at the glow of Tariel's name on her phone screen.

They all laughed softly, a quiet bond of resolve forming in the dim glow of the lamp, as the full moon outside crept closer to its destined night.

The next morning, Professor Graeves stood at the front of the high-ceilinged hall for Ancient History of Dragons, her long silver robe swishing as she gestured toward the illuminated smart board glowing with ancient glyphs. A vivid animated projection of a black three-headed dragon roared softly on one side, while another image of a regal, four-headed dragon with wings spread wide floated beside it in shimmering golden hues.

"In our last few sessions," she said, "we discussed some of the most powerful mythical dragons: the Minutez, the Abyssian Wyrm, keeper of subterranean flame, the Hell's Fire Dragon, the Celestine Drake, a sky-born sentinel who sang storms into sleep, and the Heavenly Divine Dragon. Today, we explore what ancient lore refers to as the 'Draconic Trinity.'

Everin sat upright, pen in hand, heart quietly hammering. She shot a glance toward Tariel beside her, who was already scribbling notes, brow furrowed in focus.

"The Trinity," Professor Graeves continued, "is not simply a group of powerful dragons. It's a celestial design that is a balance of force, fate, and divine will. Minutez is the wielder of precision and time. The Hell's Fire, is born of chaos and destruction. And the Heavenly Divine, which is often called Adalward, the four-headed dragon of protection and balance, is the guardian of the world gates."

One student raised a hand. "Why does the Hell's Fire Dragon have three heads, while Adalward has four?"

"An insightful question," Graeves nodded. "The three heads

of Hell's Fire represent the split forces of rage, ruin, and chaos. It's a creature not made for balance, but for annihilation. Each head moves in a different alignment, thus making it hard to control."

She turned to the smartboard projection of Adalward, tracing its outline with a digital laser pointer. "By contrast, Adalward's four heads symbolize unity: wisdom, courage, mercy, and strength. And being born not just of power but of divine intention. Legends say when all four heads speak in unison, even the storms fall silent."

Graeves went on, "The trinity must be complete when the world stands on the brink. Their roles are not interchangeable, nor accidental. But here's the mystery: no living dragon has ever identified all three incarnates at once. They awaken only when the balance is most threatened."

She tapped the image of the Trinity symbol glowing above the projected dragons, which was three interlocked spirals etched in ancient gold.

"There are prophecies," she said more quietly, "buried deep in the earliest dragon texts. They speak of a convergence when these three dragons appear within the same generation. And when they do, so too will rise the first of the Demon Lords."

The classroom stilled.

Another student, a boy from the eastern wing, raised his hand. "Do you mean the Demon Lords? I thought they were myths. Just stories to scare young hatchlings."

Professor Graeves shook her head solemnly. "Tynan, the Lord of Darkness and Chaos, is no myth. Nor are the tales of the 'Three Days of Darkness' that will precede his full arrival. The skies will burn, the waters will boil, and the gates between realms will weaken. The Trinity is supposed to be the key—either to seal him away once more… or to open the path."

A wave of murmurs rose among the students.

"So if these three rare dragons show up," someone whispered behind Everin, "does that mean the end of the world is coming?"

"Maybe not the end," said another. "But definitely the beginning of something huge."

Ameera whispered, "Maybe this is why our kind lives longer, to witness the onset of the demon era."

"They say dragon kind was created to fight the old evils," a girl near the front added. "And perhaps what we've been training for."

Everin remained silent, her eyes locked on the image of the Hell's Fire Dragon on the board. Its glowing emerald eyes stared back at her, filled with a darkness she didn't want to admit she recognized. A chill ran down her spine.

What if these weren't just legends? What if the awakening had already begun?

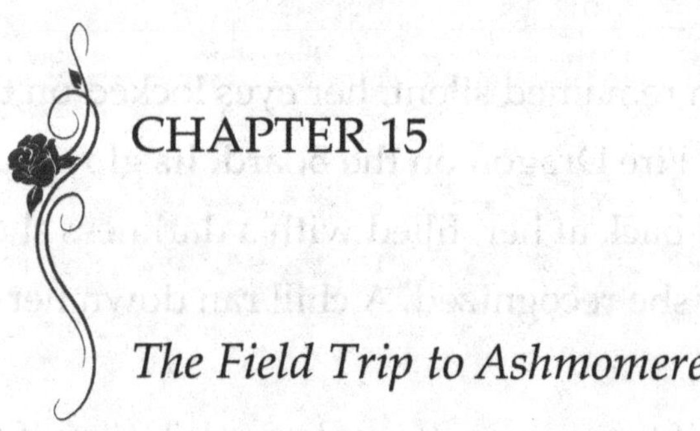

CHAPTER 15

The Field Trip to Ashmomere

About a hundred students, from wide-eyed juniors to swaggering final years, had assembled in the academy's front courtyard. The marble fountain pond at the center shimmered under the morning sun, its cascading water catching flecks of light like glittering dragon scales.

Everin adjusted the strap of her camping gear bag and trudged across the stone path, scanning the crowd until she spotted Tariya. She picked up her pace, nearly stumbling as the weight of her bag shifted.

"Someone forgot to pack light," Tariya teased, her curls bouncing as she turned.

"I didn't want to miss anything important," Everin said breathlessly.

Tariel strolled over, slinging his bag effortlessly over one shoulder. Jackson joined soon after, grinning as he adjusted his backward cap.

Phoenix, standing a few meters away, was already in full glam mode, taking selfies in perfect light, pouting with exaggerated flair while a group of first years giggled behind her.

Near one of the larger stone benches, a few senior girls were whispering and giggling behind their hands as they glanced not so subtly at Thorian Ashmore and Zale Nightwind, the two brooding final-year heartthrobs. Everin caught the words "total dragonfire" and "imagine being paired with them." She rolled her eyes and turned her attention to the gathering staff.

Professor Stark stood tall and no nonsense beside the fountain, flanked by Professor Graeves in her windswept gray cloak and the ever-looming Professor Rudiff, his arms crossed as usual. Other staff members chatted quietly, including a short, chubby professor with a chestnut beard.

"Who's that?" Everin asked, nudging Tariya. She'd seen him before in the assemblies, but never really bothered to ask about his major.

"Oh, that's Professor Vantle. Potions. We'll have him next term. Don't let the beard fool you, his lessons are like cauldron boot-camp."

Headmaster Fenwick stepped up beside the fountain, projecting authority with every word. "All students, listen up. Juniors, line up to the right. Seniors and Finals to the left. And please, tell me no one forgot their Aegisweave?"

A collective rustle followed as students tugged at their collars or tapped the fine shimmer-thread armor beneath their clothes.

Everin leaned closer to Jackson and whispered, "That's it? Just one small bus for all of us?"

Jackson smirked. "We'll fly, obviously."

Tariya laughed. "Oh, sure, and alert every news network from here to Chicago that dragons roam the countryside. Smart."

"Wait and watch, Miss Haydon," Tariel said smoothly, stepping a little closer so his shadow nearly eclipsed hers. Everin's stomach did a little flip.

Professor Stark and Graeves moved to either side of the fountain. Each student passed through the cascading water, and on the other side, with a pop, tiny dragons, no larger than a mouse, emerged in flashes of color. Scarlet, sapphire, gold, and emerald, soon the sky above was filled with fluttering baby dragons darting and diving.

Fenwick raised a shimmering scale to his lips and spoke through the amplifier. The dragons immediately snapped to attention, forming ranks in the air before diving, one by one, through the bus windows.

"Neatly now!" Professor Stark barked. "No wing scratches or tail burns!"

The professors and a few unshifted juniors, including the three late bloomers, were directed to board the small, enchanted bus. Everin had just stepped onto the first step when a cheeky first-year gawked up at Tariel.

"Wow. You're like seven feet tall and still no dragon? You sure you're not just a glorified tree?"

Everin burst into giggles as Tariel just gave the boy a slow, theatrical blink. "Only trees that breathe fire."

Everin took her seat next to the window, and Tariel took the seat next to her. Her heart skipped a beat because she didn't expect him to sit with her.

While Phoenix took the seat behind them, she said dryly, "Hopefully, a professor doesn't sit next to me."

That very moment, Professor Stark, who couldn't find a seat

elsewhere, occupied the seat next to Phoenix. Everin swore she literally saw Phoenix's face turn dark and her eyes bulge in disappointment.

Inside the bus, dragons swarmed the ceiling like a school of locusts, chirping and flapping until Headmaster Fenwick growled. Immediately, they calmed and settled onto the transparent windows like colorful ornaments.

Everin turned in awe, marveling at the living kaleidoscope above them. "This is cool, like someone had thrown specks of paint inside the bus."

"Guess there are advantages for not being able to transform," said Tariel in admiration.

Then a small coral-colored dragon, unable to balance itself on the edge of the bus window, dropped and tangled in Everin's long, dark hair.

"Ah!" she gasped and tried to free the dragon before it started spitting fire in an attempt to free itself.

"Here, let me..." Tariel leaned over, and his fingers touched hers.

Everin stilled, then quickly let go of the tiny dragon. She

leaned a bit toward Tariel to give him access to her head, and her eyes zeroed in on his neck. The nearness made her senses tingle; she could feel the warmth of him, smell the subtle cinnamon mixed with cedar that clung to his clothes.

Tariel carefully pried the dragon loose, his fingers brushing the nape of Everin's neck as he disentangled the creature.

"Easy there, flamelet," he muttered to the dragon with a grin. Then he added under his breath, "Seems you, too, like the scent of peach blossoms."

Everin's eyes widened slightly as she realized he was teasing her about the lingering scent of her shampoo. Her cheeks burned brighter than dragon fire. She mumbled a thanks, trying not to melt from the butterflies in her stomach. The moment passed, and she had to stare out the window just to remember how breathing worked.

The bus started moving, and Everin realized that tonight she would have to take the risk of sneaking out of the camp in Ashmomere.

The bus rolled to a stop on a wide stretch of hilly grassland, the soft earth dotted with wildflowers and sloping gently toward a ridge overlooking the valley below.

A flurry of color and light burst from the bus as the school of tiny dragons fluttered out, soaring high above the meadow before swirling down in spirals. Everin quickly pulled out her phone and captured the breathtaking display, dragons trailing shimmering wings against the vast sky, the peaks and trees forming a picture-perfect backdrop.

She watched in fascination as each dragon shimmered mid-air, then reverted to human form upon landing, their bags still strapped securely. Some coughed, others staggered with dizzy expressions, especially the wide-eyed juniors.

"Boys to the east! Follow me," barked Professor Vantle.

"Girls, this way!" called Professor Graeves, already directing them west across the open field.

Everin followed Tariya and Phoenix to a patch of soft grass and began unrolling her tent. The buzz of conversation, laughter, and flapping canvas filled the air as dozens of tents rose under the warm midday sun.

Once the tents were pitched and gear stowed, the professors gathered them again. The short hike into town took only a few minutes. Everin stuck close to her friends, her eyes widening as they passed through the streets of Ashmomere.

The town looked picturesque, with cobbled streets winding between steep-roofed stone cottages. Decorative banners flapped in the breeze, deep crimson, gold, and sapphire, each adorned with sigils of moons, dragons, and swirling flame motifs. Props for the upcoming Moonlight Revels had been arranged along the main road: glowing paper lanterns shaped like phoenixes and scaled creatures, garlands of enchanted ivy twisting up lampposts, and a stage being erected near the town square.

Decorative iron lanterns hung beneath timber awnings, casting playful patterns on the cobbled path. A small clock tower stood proudly at the center, its weathered face displaying the time in elegant brass numerals, soft mechanical chimes echoing through the afternoon air.

Warm, woodsy scents wafted from open bakery windows, blending with the rich tang of roasted spices from food stalls already prepping for the evening. Hand-painted signs with dragon crests and fiery flourishes swung gently above shop doors.

"Wow, they've really gone all out," Everin said, taking in the vibrant decorations strung across the street, lanterns shaped like miniature dragons, streamers fluttering in the mountain breeze, and wooden stalls being dressed with glowing crystals and fabric swags.

Phoenix grinned. "Moonlight Revels, baby. Told you it was going to be a thing."

"We knew it'd be festive," Everin replied, "but this looks like something out of a fantasy movie."

"It is a fantasy movie. We're living it," Tariya said dryly, glancing around. "According to the town's site, the mayor's been planning this for weeks. And the competition's the highlight tonight."

Phoenix bounced slightly in her boots. "I swear, if it's fashion-themed or dancing, I'm going full Bevington charm."

"I bet it would be singing or dancing," Tariya confirmed, scrolling through her phone. "I've researched Ashmomere's past festivals, and usually it's impromptu performances. Locals and visitors would both be allowed to compete."

"Ugh, now I wish I'd brought heels," Phoenix muttered, eyeing the cobbled road as if it had offended her. Then she added with a sly grin, "Guess we are shopping."

Everin chuckled, but her gaze lingered on the decorations, the magic, the people, the buzz of celebration. Something told her tonight would be anything but ordinary.

Once they reached the town square, Headmaster Fenwick turned and addressed the students. "You have three hours," he announced. "Explore respectfully, and if you're returning to the tents to change for the evening, inform a professor. Tonight's dinner will be held at Embergrill Tavern, and then we'll head to the Town Hall for the Moonlight Revels. Attendance is mandatory, and punctuality is not optional."

A ripple of excitement surged through the students, many of whom immediately began chatting about the event.

Everin lingered for a moment, eyes on the bright stage being prepared in the square, her thoughts already dancing ahead to what the evening might bring.

CHAPTER 16

The Moonlight Revel

The full moon rose high above Ashmomere, casting silver light over the town's stone rooftops and cobbled streets. Lanterns floated through the air like drifting stars, while the music that echoed from the town square was lively, enchanted, and impossibly beautiful.

After a hearty dinner at Embergrill Tavern, where the long tables groaned under platters of flame-grilled meats and roasted vegetables, the Academy students were ushered out in a cheerful procession. Laughter and music echoed through the town's winding alleys as they followed glowing streetlamps toward the next block, where the real spectacle awaited.

The Ashmomere Town Hall had been transformed. Lanterns of every hue bobbed overhead, suspended by magic, casting soft ripples of color across the stone-paved square. Enchanted flower petals rained down like confetti, vanishing before they touched the ground. Musicians stood ready at the grand arched entrance, tuning instruments that hovered and glowed. Everin stepped into the square, eyes wide at the full sweep of the festival.

The Moonlight Revels were in full swing, with fire dancers twirling on raised stages, illusionists conjuring tiny dragons made of smoke, and vendors offering glittering sweets shaped like scaled fruit. The air buzzed with magic and festivities.

And yet, beneath the shimmering lights and the cheer of her classmates, a knot of unease tightened in Everin's stomach.

When is this going to end? she thought, glancing at the moon rising steadily in the darkening sky. We still have to find the Emberroot, and time's running out.

A secret mission tugged at the edge of her thoughts. They had come to Ashmomere for more than just the festival. Hidden beneath the joy and celebration was something more urgent, more dangerous. Something only five of them knew.

Everin didn't know how long the event would last or how long they would have after that. But she couldn't afford to miss the full moon.

Somewhere in the shadows beyond the festival lights, Ember-root waited.

And so did everything that came with it.

Everin stood beside Tariya and Phoenix somewhere in the middle of the crowd in the grand town hall, watching the steady flow of townsfolk and Academy students file inside. The whole square glittered with ribbons of magic light and blooming petals that floated without wind.

Phoenix, dressed in a flowing silver wrap dress threaded with glittering sequins, caught every lantern beam as if it belonged to her. Diamond-shaped earrings swayed with her every toss of hair, and her silver heels clicked smartly against the polished floor as though the entire hall were her runway.

Tariya wore a fitted dark-green dress with sharp, simple lines. Everin had gone for a black long-sleeved top tucked into a skirt, paired with stockings and boots. Her hair hung loose around her shoulders, with the barest touch of makeup to soften her features.

"So… we are really doing this?" Phoenix asked, lips curving.

Tariya rolled her eyes. "We've already known about the Moonlight Revels for a week. You've been planning your outfit since Tuesday."

Everin spotted a familiar woman entering the hall, tall, commanding, with a platinum braid and the Council's insignia on her cloak. It was Mariah Mac Naught, Chief of the Dragon Council of the West. The mayor and Headmaster Fenwick moved quickly to greet her, ushering her to a place of honor near the stage.

"Looks like she's really watching us," came Tariel's voice near Everin's ear, so close she jumped slightly.

The five of them, Everin, Tariya, Phoenix, Tariel, and Jackson, drifted forward with the crowd. The master of ceremonies raised his voice through a glittering dragon scale amplifier.

"Ladies and gentlemen, citizens of Ashmomere and visiting students of the Drakon Academy! This year's Moonlight Revel committee is proud to announce that tonight's celebration will feature a surprise competition!"

Phoenix clutched Tariya's arm. "Please, please let it be make-up."

"A dance competition!" the MC declared with flourish.

Phoenix groaned. "So close."

But before the laughter in the crowd could settle, the mayor stepped forward. In his hands he carried a gleaming shield, unlike any prize Everin had ever seen. Its frame was gold, carved with dragon sigils that glowed faintly in the moonlight. And inset into the center, resting in delicate crystal sockets, were vials of rare liquids that shimmered with their own inner light.

Gasps rippled through the crowd. Near the front of the square, a long table had been set up where a panel of judges, three robed officials from the Council, and two local dignitaries from Ashmomere sat, their expressions sharp with interest as they leaned forward to examine the prize.

"This," the mayor announced, raising the shield high, "is the Ashmomere Moonlight Shield. A treasure of our town. It carries within it gifts most rare. Six vials, each a boon beyond measure. One," he pointed, "is Veilvine Sap, harvested from the cliffs of Aether Gorge under a full eclipse. Another," he gestured to a vial glowing silver-blue, "is Lumerial Essence, known for breaking through even the strongest layers of enchantment and barriers."

The audience murmured, some in awe, others gasping outright. "Impossible," someone whispered nearby. "No one parts with Lumerial Essence. It can strip wards older than kingdoms."

Everin's pulse skipped. Veilvine Sap. The very thing they had read about in the library, one of the elixir's ingredients. Her eyes darted to Tariel, then to Tariya, and then to Phoenix. The realization struck them all at once.

Phoenix leaned in, voice sharp with excitement. "That's it. That's what we need."

Everin glanced at the final-year girls, Selene Veyra was among them, all poised and confident in their glittering gowns. Her throat tightened. "Can we really dance well enough to win against them?" she whispered.

Jackson muttered under his breath, his gaze still locked on the shield. "We've to try at least, that vial changes everything."

Tariel exhaled slowly, lips curving in a grin. "Guess that means we dance." And before anyone could stop him, he slipped into the crowd, angling toward the open circle.

Tariya, who had been inching backward toward the safety of the benches, suddenly squeaked as Jackson gave her a not-so-gentle push from behind. She stumbled into the light of the circle, arms flailing. "Jackson!" she hissed.

"Oh no, Miss Gamer," he said with mock solemnity, folding his arms. "You're not hiding tonight."

Everin's stomach flipped. This was happening.

The music struck up, an enchanted blend of waltz, contemporary, and salsa, shifting in rhythm with the drumbeats. All around the square, the space was cleared, forming a grand open circle under the enchanted lanterns.

People began pairing off. Some were drawn by charm magic, others by eager hands. One of the final-year girls tried to claim Zale Nightwind, but Phoenix tripped her "accidentally" in the crowd and swept in to take his hand before anyone could blink.

They were good. Phoenix threw in sleek modern twirls, and Zale kept up with a mix of swagger and old-school flair. The crowd whooped in delight.

Headmaster Fenwick gave Everin a gentle push forward, his beard twinkling as if he knew exactly what he was doing. "Miss Haydon, I believe you owe us a dance."

And waiting in the middle of the floor, smirking, hand outstretched, was Tariel.

"Oh, stars," she whispered, her heart stuttering.

She took his hand, hesitant but unable to resist. He drew her in with an easy pull, his palm warm against hers.

Their first steps were clumsy. Everin's boot caught his toe, and she hissed an apology. But Tariel only chuckled and slid an arm around her waist, steadying her. The heat of his touch sent a shiver racing through her. She looked up, and for a heartbeat too long, her gaze caught his.

He spun her, and her hair fanned out, her skirt swirling as she turned. As she twirled back into his hold, her eyes darted across the square. She caught sight of Thorian Ashmore's partner, Selene, a tall final-year girl in a glittering gown. She was graceful at first, until her tight dress betrayed her. On a sharp turn, she stumbled badly, her heel catching on the floorboard, and went down hard. The judges exchanged a look and, with regret, disqualified her. Thorian's scowl was thunderous.

Across the circle, Jackson was attempting to guide Tariya into something resembling rhythm. She moved stiffly, like a reluctant mannequin being dragged across the floor, her glare fixed firmly on him. The crowd chuckled, and Jackson, grinning, leaned in with an exaggerated flourish. "Come on, give them your best." Tariya shot him a death stare, stomped once in deliberate protest, then spun herself in motion and almost slapped Jackson with her deadly spin. Everin nearly laughed out loud, though she quickly bit it back as Tariel swept her into another turn.

Tariel drew Everin closer, and her breath caught. His movements were smoother than she expected, confident, and sure. He guided her through another turn, and her eyes landed on an elderly dragon couple gliding across the circle. Their steps were slow, dignified, like a memory of centuries past. The crowd clapped softly in rhythm, enchanted by their grace.

Then the tempo shifted.

The Firestep began. The drums pounded harder, the rhythm older and wilder than anything before. Sparks leapt in the air, as though the music itself had teeth. Couples all around quickened their pace. Phoenix and Zale matched it effortlessly, their dance sharper, flashier, winning over the crowd.

The elderly couple faltered. They smiled at each other, bowed, and stepped aside, breathless but proud.

Tariya, on the other hand, leaned fully into her oddball routine. Her limbs flailed in stiff, jerky angles, her face impassive as if she was utterly bored with the whole ordeal. The crowd laughed again, some clapping along, others whispering. But when Jackson, exasperated, backed off the circle altogether, Tariya shrugged, gave one last bizarre twirl, and strutted out like she owned the floor. The judges signaled her out, but she tossed her long hair and left with zero shame, still swaying to her own rhythm. Everin caught herself grinning even as she spun back into Tariel's arms.

Everin's pulse raced. She fought to keep up with Tariel's lead as he spun her again. She stumbled, but his grip was firm, grounding her. Together they found the rhythm, their bodies moving as if pulled by something deeper than the music.

Then their fingers brushed again, and everything shifted.

A shimmer pulsed where their hands met. Golden dragon light traced up Everin's wrist, mirrored in the same glow flaring across Tariel's arm. With every beat of the Firestep drums, the light brightened, burning hotter, wrapping tighter.

Gasps rose through the crowd. Dancers faltered. The elderly couple, who had moments before been gliding with such poise, slowed to a halt, their faces lit with awe. One by one, the other pairs stilled, until only Phoenix and Zale kept dancing, along with Everin and Tariel. The music thundered on, the drums pounding, but the square itself had fallen into hush.

"What's happening?" someone cried from the edge of the circle.

"That's a Bonding Glow!" another voice shouted.

Everin's chest tightened as the energy coursed through her, ancient and undeniable. Her body moved as if it were no longer hers, every step drawn to Tariel's, every turn sharpened by the rhythm. The glow pulsed between them, hot, alive, unrelenting. For a moment she forgot the square, the festival, the crowd. There was only him.

The elderly woman who had stepped aside pressed a hand to her chest, her voice trembling as it carried into the hush. "Few ever show the Bonding Glow. It is said to bind two dragons whose hearts are joined by the truest love. The stars and the abyss both curse it. It is a bond tested by sacrifice, where one must be willing to give everything for the other."

Whispers rippled outward, awe mixing with fear.

Everin's pulse hammered. She could not look away from Tariel. The enchantment wrapped around them, pulling them tighter, faster, until suddenly something changed.

Tariel's grip stiffened. His steps faltered. His eyes flickered an unnatural blue.

"Tariel?" Everin whispered.

His gaze was distant, cold. Sweat beaded across his brow.

Tariel wasn't in the town hall anymore.

He was flying, no, falling, through a dark sky. Flames licked at his thoughts. A dragon with emerald eyes and blackened wings loomed in the abyss, its smirk cruel and all-knowing.

It wanted control.

The beat of the drums pounded in his chest, not music anymore, but chains. He clenched his jaw, fighting it.

No. Not here. Not now.

He pushed Everin away gently. "Break the bond," he croaked. She stumbled back in confusion.

Then, with a trembling hand, Tariel raised his arm and shouted a single word that rang through the hall like thunder: "Solivern!"

A wave of shimmering force blasted from his palm. The spell struck the enchanted instruments. The drums cracked mid-beat and went silent. Petals froze mid-air.

The force sent Everin stumbling back, her eyes wide with

shock.

And everything stopped.

Gasps rippled through the crowd. Even the mayor rose to his feet.

From the back, an old woman whispered, "That is an elder dragon's Severance Spell. No one has spoken it in thousands of years…"

Others began murmuring at once.

A man in dark robes shook his head. "Impossible."

Professor Greaves adjusted her spectacles, muttering, "I have only ever seen the word in fragments of forgotten scrolls."

An elderly woman clutched her shawl tighter. "Only gods or demons would dare speak such a curse."

Another voice rose from the crowd, uncertain and fearful. "No one even knows how it is performed. How does this boy know it?"

Tariel's pulse thundered. He could feel eyes on him from every corner of the hall.

High above, Mariah Mac Naught leaned forward in her seat, her silver-streaked braid catching the lantern light. Her gaze locked on him, sharp and unyielding, as though weighing his very soul. Tariel stiffened under the weight of it.

Beside the stage, one of the elderly council scribes muttered, "This is beyond recorded incantations. Such words do not simply surface."

Headmaster Fenwick, standing among the faculty, spoke quickly, his tone deceptively light though his jaw was tight. "He reads too many ancient texts," Fenwick said to the scribe, forcing a thin smile. "Perhaps he decided to experiment. Boys and their impulses."

But Tariel caught the way his father's eyes betrayed unease. He knew it was no accident. His hands still trembled. The glow on his arms faded. His breath came in ragged bursts.

The judges exchanged glances. Mariah's eyes narrowed, sharp and calculating.

"Disqualified," one judge announced softly.

The spell lifted and the music returned.

Tariel felt Everin's gaze on him. When he looked up, she asked softly, "Are you alright?"

"Yes," he said, then added, "I'm sorry. I didn't mean to push you. It just… happened."

"It's okay," she replied.

Only one pair remained, Phoenix and Zale.

They spun into their final pose, the crowd erupting in cheers as Phoenix flipped her hair and dipped with flair. Zale gave a dramatic bow, soaking up the applause.

The mayor stepped forward, lifting the dragon-forged shield inlaid with glowing glass vials. The onlookers murmured again, the light from the vials catching in every eye.

Tariel stood among the students, watching as Phoenix strode forward like she owned the square. She lingered for the festival photographers, tossing her braid over one shoulder, flashing her signature smile, and spinning once for added effect. Zale matched her step for step, grinning with arrogant ease.

Tariel stayed close to Everin as Phoenix finally turned away from the cameras and approached. Without a word, Phoenix held out one of the vials, its bluish glow casting a faint shimmer across Everin's face.

"Veilvine Sap," Phoenix said, her voice calm but her grin irrepressible. "Exactly what we need. We actually did it."

Everin blinked, clearly startled. "Yes, and you won it."

"Correction," Zale cut in smoothly as he strolled over, brows raised. "We won. I was part of that performance too."

Phoenix rolled her eyes, thrusting the shield with the rest of the vials into his arms. "Fine. Take the lot, Nightwind. You earned it."

Then she lifted the single vial again, turning back to Everin. Her smile softened, almost conspiratorial. "But this one's mine to give. You know what to do with it."

Tariel watched as Everin's fingers closed around the glass. He felt the weight of that moment settle in his chest. One ingredient down. Only two remained.

Before he could speak, movement caught his eye. His father, headmaster Fenwick was crossing the floor with urgency, his robes trailing behind him. He reached Tariel and put a firm hand on his shoulder.

"Are you all right?" Fenwick's voice was low.

Tariel straightened. "Yes, Dad, I'm fine."

Senior Fenwick's breath hitched. "That was… a Severance Spell?" His father's brows knit.

"Not now," Tariel said quickly, his voice sharper than he intended. Too many eyes were still on them. Too many whispers.

Fenwick's jaw tightened, but he nodded. "All right. We will not speak of it here. But come home when you are ready to talk. Your mother and I will be waiting."

Tariel swallowed hard and gave the smallest of nods. The word still burned on his tongue. Solivern.

He did not know where it had come from. He only knew that something inside him had spoken it.

And that terrified him more than anything.

CHAPTER 17

Spores, Fire Moths, and Secrets

The full moon hung high in the night sky, casting a silver sheen over the Ashmomere ridge and the darkened tents below.

Tucked behind the farthest row of tents, just beyond the reach of the last lantern's glow, three figures huddled in the shadows, careful to keep their voices low. From this angle, no professors had a direct line of sight. That was the point.

Phoenix stood with her arms folded and a dramatic huff, her silvery-pink fluffy jacket shimmering faintly under the moonlight. Glitter makeup dusted her lids, and glossy boots peeked from beneath her cuffed trousers. She looked more like she was about to step onto a floating stage than into a forest of fire moths.

Tariya squinted at her in disbelief. "Are we sneaking out," she whispered, adjusting her black hoodie, "or attending a forest fashion gala?"

Phoenix shot her a smug look, then posed with an exaggerated shoulder tilt. "Preparation," she mouthed with theatrical flair. "If I'm going to get dirt on me, I'd rather look flawless doing it."

Everin clamped a hand over her mouth to stifle a laugh.

"She's going to alert every moth in a ten-mile radius," Tariya muttered behind a smirk, pulling her curls into a low bun.

"Shh," Everin whispered, glancing toward the rest of the sleeping camp. A few snoring sounds floated from nearby tents. "Keep it down."

The girls shifted closer into the dark, careful not to rustle too many leaves underfoot.

Then, Everin turned slightly toward Phoenix. "Hey," she said in a hushed voice, "thanks for earlier. For winning and trusting me with the Veilvine sap."

Phoenix grinned. "Please. The mayor said Veilvine Sap was part of the prize, and we late bloomers need it. That elixir won't make itself. We're in this together."

Tariya's eyebrows rose. "Isn't it a bit too much of a coincidence that you won the Veilvine sap exactly when you badly needed it?"

Phoenix rolled her eyes. "Zale won the shield too, remember? He can have the rest of the potions. I told him, 'You take the lot, but this one's mine to take.'"

Everin smiled, then blinked in surprise when Tariya leaned in a little closer, her voice dropping even lower. "You and Tariel," she said, "you... glowed."

Phoenix nodded eagerly. "Bonding glow. Not subtle."

Everin's face warmed instantly. "It wasn't—it just happened. I wasn't expecting anything."

"Neither was the room," Phoenix whispered with a quiet giggle. "Also, that spell he cast? What was it—Solivern?"

"An elder dragon's Severance Spell," Tariya whispered. "That was powerful magic. People have only heard of that spell. No one really knows how to cast it. It's ancient lost magic."

Before Everin could respond, a soft crunch of footsteps behind them made them all go still.

Two figures emerged quietly from behind a nearby tree. Tariel, midnight-blue jacket zipped halfway up, looked calm and focused. Jackson wore a gray hoodie and rubbed his eyes like he'd just woken up from a nap he didn't approve of.

"Are we sneaking out," Jackson mumbled, "or is there a moonlight fashion pageant?"

Phoenix flipped her braid, eyes glittering. "Jealousy is such a bad color on you, Jackson."

Tariel gave Everin a small nod, eyes scanning the slope ahead. "You ready?"

Everin secured the sapphire shaft across her back, exhaled slowly, and nodded. "Let's go."

The five students grouped together behind the last row of tents. Tariel pulled a crystal pendant from under his shirt and murmured a cloaking incantation. A thin, misty veil shimmered over them, rendering their forms nearly invisible in the moonlight.

The entire campsite was warded with a protective dragon enchantment. Anyone crossing its edge without permission would trigger an alarm or shimmer burst to alert the professors. As they approached the invisible perimeter, Everin's breath caught. One more step and they would either be caught or be clear.

Tariel leaned toward Everin and whispered, "Let's hope the cloak holds. Crossing this barrier without a ripple will be our miracle."

They stepped through.

Nothing.

No shimmer. No siren. No burst of light.

"The cloak works," Tariya whispered, glancing back.

They moved silently through the trees, moonlight casting silvery shadows over the forest floor. From behind them, Everin thought she saw movement. Professor Stark. Her pale cloak drifted between tents as she paced the area, looking distracted. For a moment, Everin could have sworn Stark paused and looked directly at them. But then she turned away.

They kept moving.

Down the winding trail past the trees, a faint glowing spore path began to emerge, soft blue and green motes of light hanging in the air like floating pollen. It guided them through the dark underbrush until the terrain sloped upward. Ash-momere's volcanic ridge loomed ahead, its jagged rocks glowing faintly red in the distance.

"This is the place," Tariya whispered, checking her notes.

A sudden hiss made them freeze.

Dozens of winged creatures swirled from the ridge, fiery orange moths with ember-glowing wings. They pulsed with heat and glared with too many eyes.

"Fire moths," Tariel muttered.

"Of course, it can't be as easy as just picking up a herb and going back," Jackson added sarcastically.

The moths moved aggressively, protecting the charred clearing where a single strange plant glowed from the soil.

"No transforming," Tariel added quietly. "If anyone shifts, the professors will sense it instantly, even if we are a mile away from them. Stay human."

Everin felt her breath catch. That had to be the Feathered Emberroot.

"Hold them back," she whispered. "I can feel it. I know where to dig."

The moths launched. Tariel deflected a burst of flame with a flick of his sapphire shaft. Jackson, spotting a winged blur near Phoenix, darted in front, but was quickly overwhelmed by the swarm. While backtracking, he fell.

Phoenix's fluffy sleeve caught a scorch, and she let out a shriek.

"My jacket!"

She raised her shaft and, with a sharp yell, thrust it forward. A sudden pulse of energy erupted from the tip, flaring in a circular blast. Several moths dropped from the sky, stunned. She stared in disbelief.

Jackson, picking himself up, gaped. "That was amazing."

Phoenix blinked. "I didn't even know I could do that."

"Do it again!" he grinned.

With renewed fire, Phoenix slashed through the air, her shaft blazing. Tariya joined in, shouting over the screeches of the moths. They moved in a tight circle, shafts whirling, blasts of power colliding with flaming wings.

Everin dropped to her knees. She could feel a strange vibration beneath the earth, like the plant was calling to her. Carefully, using her gloves, she dug around the glowing stalk.

"Everin! Hurry!" Tariya yelled, barely dodging a burst of fire.

More moths swarmed. A huge cluster. Everin shielded her face, heart racing. Just a few more seconds, and she could get the root.

Tariel saw Everin hunched over the soil, her gloved hands trembling as she reached for the root. Moths burst toward her like flaming arrows.

His grip on the shaft tightened.

No way was he letting her get hurt.

Power surged from deep within. Without thinking, he stepped forward and raised the shaft. Boom! A pulse of light erupted, a spiraling burst of pure energy that cut through the air.

The moths froze. Wings halted mid-beat. They hung in the air like stunned fireflies caught in stillness.

Tariya, wide-eyed, stumbled back. "That was… high-order dragon casting. Only experienced elder dragons can do that."

Tariel had no idea how he managed such a strong spell, yet again. Earlier, during the dance, it was the Spell of Severance, and now this pure burst of energy. Anyway, he didn't have time to think about these spells now. All he knew was that he wanted to protect his friends, especially the girl crouched beside him. Now relieved, his gaze rested on Everin.

She reached into the earth and pulled the Emberroot plant, its feathers glowing brightly.

"Got it!"

"We need to go—now!" he barked.

The five of them bolted through the trees, the glowing spore path lighting their way. Behind them, the moths still hung suspended, but not for long.

They crossed the warded perimeter once more.

Still no shimmer. No alarm.

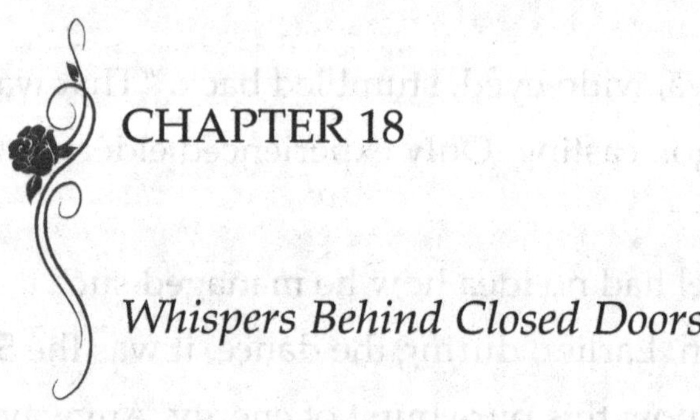

CHAPTER 18

Whispers Behind Closed Doors

Sunday morning brought a rare quiet over Drakon Academy. The campus felt slower, drowsier, as sunlight spilled through glass-paneled halls and the spires cast long shadows on the lawn.

Tariel made his way toward the Headmaster's quarters, separated from the rest of the school by a stretch of runed hedges and a narrow stone path that few students ever had reason to follow. The building itself was old but elegant, with arched windows, carved lintels shaped like curling dragon tails, and a small tower that rose just above the tree line.

The house always felt half like a home and half like a council office. Which, for the Fenwicks, it was.

As soon as he pushed open the front door, a voice rang out from deeper inside.

"There you are!" his mother called. "I've been waiting since breakfast!"

She swept into the foyer in her usual long-sleeved dress, forest green today, with her auburn curls piled in a loose twist. Isolde Fenwick, a diplomat, council envoy, and an expert in giving Tariel guilt with just one look.

"You didn't call or send a message, nothing."

"I was going to..."

"Your father has been pacing like a storm dragon with a broken wing," she added, and Tariel couldn't help the laugh that escaped.

Headmaster Fenwick appeared behind her, still in his weekend sweater and dragonhide slippers. "Welcome home, son. We need to talk."

That sentence instantly made Tariel straighten.

They ushered him into the living room, where logs crackled softly in the hearth and an enchanted kettle poured tea into three mismatched mugs. The space smelled of oakwood, old parchment, and something faintly citrusy, his mother's favorite calming charm.

His father leaned forward, fingers steepled. "Let's not dance around it. The spell you cast during the Moonlight Revel, how did you do it?"

Tariel hesitated. "I didn't know what I was doing. I swear."

"You cast Solivern," Isolde said quietly. "That's not a classroom spell. That's ancient, pre-Era magic. Most historians don't even know what it does."

"I didn't know it either," Tariel replied. "We were dancing… and then something shifted. I felt like I was being pulled into something. Like someone was trying to take over."

"Someone?" his father asked sharply.

"A dragon," Tariel said slowly. "Or something that looked like one. Massive. Green-eyed. I don't know if it was real or just in my head, but it was watching me. Smirking. Like it knew something I didn't."

He paused, remembering the pressure in his chest, the pounding drums, the flash of the spell that had poured out of him like instinct.

"I just knew I had to break away from it. And that word Solivern just came from somewhere deep inside. I didn't think. I just... said it."

Isolde and Fenwick exchanged a look.

His father finally leaned back with a sigh. "Well, continue with your meditations. Hopefully, you can transform into your dragon form soon, and all other ancient magic talk will die once people see that you are a normal dragon."

Tariel gave a faint nod.

Later, as he stepped upstairs toward his room, he caught their voices again, which were low and almost hesitant.

"Do you think he's the one?" Isolde asked.

"The one the Council suspects is coming?" his father replied. "The feared one... God forbid, no! You know what can happen if anyone even suspects a little that he's the feared one."

Tariel's heart thudded as he closed his door.

The feared one?

Whatever was stirring inside him... it wasn't done yet.

The next morning, fog rolled across the Drakon Academy courtyards like lazy smoke, curling around towers and disappearing into the sky. The high ceilings in the eastern wing glowed softly with magical lights and illusions.

Students filtered into Professor Graeves' lecture amphitheater which was a brilliant fusion of arcane charm and modern utility. Floating parchments flitted above their desks, projecting summaries and historical keywords. But at the front and center stood a sleek obsidian smartboard, rune-etched and humming softly with magical energy.

Tariel took a seat in the last row beside Phoenix, who was halfway through twisting her braid into a high knot. In front of them, Everin, Tariya, and Jackson leaned in toward each other, their voices hushed under the ambient classroom buzz.

"We've got two ingredients down," Everin murmured, tapping the glowing glyph-pad in front of her. "Emberroot and Veilvine sap."

"Which leaves only one," said Tariya in a whisper. "Alpha Dragon Dust."

Jackson raised an eyebrow. "Which… we still have no clue how to find."

"Not exactly," Everin said, glancing around before lowering her voice. "I've been reading. The dust has to come from Braskora."

"Braskora?" Phoenix repeated from behind them, keeping her voice low. "That's a dragon name I've never heard of."

"He was an Alpha," Everin said. "Legendary class. Supposedly still dormant. Somewhere close."

The lights dimmed suddenly—the smartboard came alive with a luminous shimmer as Professor Graeves glided in. Her coat today was embroidered with sharp silver thread, shaped into ancient sigils and house crests. She dropped her runed tablet onto the desk and immediately synced it to the board.

"Let's begin," she said crisply. "Our topic: The High Bindings of the Eastern Reaches. And the dragons who shaped the First Accord."

The screen displayed a sweeping map of pre-Council territories, flanked by moving images of dragon clans and treaty seals. Names such as Verdanthorne, Marrask, and Emberveil floated beside their sigils.

Everin glanced back at Tariel, who gave a small nod.

Tariel raised his hand.

Graeves glanced up. "Yes, Mr. Fenwick?"

"Professor, is it true there was an Alpha dragon named Braskora?"

The room stilled, interested.

Graeves tapped her rune-tablet. A new slide flickered onto the smartboard: a massive dragon curled in a sleeping coil, scales dark emerald with veins of obsidian, wings tucked against a body that shimmered faintly with residual magic.

"Braskora," she said. "An Alpha-class dragon. Male. Estimated age: four thousand years. Served in both the Caldrith War and the Shard Accord. Known for his ability to cancel enchantments and stabilize wild elemental zones."

Images of ancient battlegrounds flashed on the screen. Then Braskora appeared mid-flight, moving through storm clouds with a group of smaller dragons following in formation.

Tariya leaned forward slightly. "What happened to him?"

"His body reached critical magical saturation a century ago," Graeves replied. "Rather than fade or lose control, he chose ritual dormancy. He rests now beneath Drakon Academy, in the Sanctum Caverns, where his magic still helps power the school's protective charms."

There were murmurs throughout the room.

"Wait, he's here?" Jackson whispered.

Graeves gave a knowing smile. "Yes. Quite deep below the campus. The area is warded, restricted, and monitored by the Council. Braskora sleeps, and in doing so, he continues to serve."

Phoenix raised her hand, eyes wide. "Are there any living dragons connected to him?"

Another flick of her fingers brought up a family crest: a silver spiral over midnight-blue, surrounded by five stars.

"The Nightwind family is one of the few lineages that trace direct ancestry to Braskora," Graeves said. "The connection is well-documented and publicly known. It's part of why the family holds such influence across the western territories."

Everin shot a glance at Tariya and then at Phoenix.

"And yes," Graeves added, her eyes scanning the students,

"Zale Nightwind is part of that same line. The Braskora bloodline is known for strong elemental magic, particularly air and storm channeling."

Phoenix mouthed, "Of course he is," and slumped dramatically against her desk.

Tariel exchanged a look with Everin.

"And if anyone plans to trespass into the Sanctum Caverns," Graeves said dryly, "do be aware there are three layers of protective enchantments and Council wards are in place. You'd be obliterated before you reached the second barrier."

Several students chuckled nervously.

Graeves returned to her primary lecture, moving into the treaties of the First Accord.

Tariel's thoughts were filled with getting the last ingredient for the elixir. And the ancient beast that slept beneath their feet.

The library smelled of dust, parchment, and faint candle-wax. Tariel trailed behind Everin, Jackson, Phoenix, and Tariya as they wove through the aisles, pretending to be deep in casual chatter. But his mind was sharp, focused. They'd already agreed over lunch: sit close enough, talk just loudly enough, and make sure Zale Nightwind couldn't ignore them.

Sure enough, there he was. Zale lounged at one of the long tables near the stained-glass windows, posture too perfect, silver hair streaked with light pink falling into his eyes in that calculated, aristocratic way. Beside him sat Thorian Ashmore, broad-shouldered and smug as always, and Selene Veyra, the girl who always dressed as if she were about to do a ramp walk. Their books were spread wide, though none of them looked like they were reading.

Tariel led his group deliberately to the table just behind theirs. He dropped into the chair with a loud scrape of wood against stone. Phoenix followed, flipping her hair back as though she hadn't noticed Zale's raised eyebrow.

"Did you know," Tariel began in a low, conspiratorial tone, "that Braskora still breathes under the Academy?"

Everin leaned forward with a serious nod, playing along. Jackson lowered his voice like he was part of a secret plan. Tariya tapped her quill against her notes as if irritated, though Tariel could see the glint of calculation in her eyes. They were all in on it.

"Alpha-class dragon," Tariel continued, letting his voice carry just enough, "the kind that could shatter a battleground with a single roar. His magic alone powers the school's wards. And everyone knows there's only one way in."

Phoenix arched a brow. "Through the barriers."

"Three layers thick," Jackson added, tapping his book. "Council wards. Nobody could get through."

Tariel gave a slow smile. "Nobody… unless they had Lumerial Essence."

He didn't need to look. He could feel Zale stiffen behind him.

Phoenix sighed dramatically, loud enough to be heard. "Still kicking myself for not snatching that vial from the shield when I won at the Moonlight Revel. Zale got the whole lot handed to him. Lucky, smug…" she cut herself off with a bitter smile, clearly enjoying the performance.

The silence that followed was sharp enough to cut glass. Tariel let it hang. One second. Two. Three.

Then Zale's voice came, dripping with disdain. "You don't know what you're talking about, Fenwick."

Tariel turned lazily, like he'd only just noticed them sitting there. "Don't I? You're the one carrying it, aren't you? The Lumerial Essence from the Revel. The only thing that could slice through wards old as Braskora's cavern."

Selene gave a soft, scandalized laugh. Thorian leaned forward, his smile wolfish. But Zale's eyes flickered, just for a moment, and Tariel caught it. That tiny flash of truth.

"Even if I did," Zale said coolly, "you wouldn't be worthy of it. You think Braskora would stir for the likes of you? You? A would-be final year dumped with the seniors because you can't even shift?"

Tariel's jaw tightened, but he forced himself to smirk. "Guess we'll see. Tonight's the only night it can happen anyway. My father said that a waning gibbous moon weakens the charm. If anyone wants to reach Braskora, this is it."

Zale leaned forward, his voice dropping low. "Watch me, Fenwick. I'll bring a recording of my ancestor himself if I have to. I'll show you Braskora. And you'll choke on your words when I'm standing where you never could."

Tariel gave a casual shrug, as if the exchange meant nothing. But inside, his thoughts burned. *Yes. Take the bait. Open the gates. Use the Essence. Do what we can't.*

Beside him, Everin shifted uneasily, but Tariel didn't meet her eyes. He couldn't. This was risky, maybe reckless, but it was the only chance they had.

CHAPTER 19

Beneath the Academy

The air in the underground levels of Drakon Academy felt older than time. It carried a stillness that pressed against Everin's skin, like the whole world was holding its breath beneath the school's foundations. The arc-lanterns embedded into the stone walls flickered with pale blue light, casting long shadows across the moss-lined corridors as they walked deeper into the depths of the academy.

Everin kept close to the others, Tariel in front, map in hand, the rest trailing behind in silence.

"Are you absolutely sure this is the right path?" she asked, her voice a whisper. "We've passed that same chipped column twice."

Tariel didn't turn around. "I got the map from Fenwick's office."

Everin narrowed her eyes. "Got it… or stole it?"

"Borrowed. Briefly. Without permission." He shrugged. "Semantics."

Jackson snorted. Phoenix rolled her eyes. Tariya just looked mildly impressed.

The tunnel dipped into a wider corridor carved with old sigils. Everin felt her pulse pick up. A shimmer floated just ahead, a massive arched gateway laced with three glistening layers of protective charms.

"Found it," Tariel murmured.

Everin took a cautious step forward. Professor Graeves had mentioned the barriers, the kind that protected something ancient, something powerful. She was about to ask if he saw a way through when a low murmur of voices drifted from the passage beside them.

She tensed.

They weren't alone.

"I hope it's who we are expecting is coming," she whispered, stepping back into the shadows.

Footsteps echoed on the stone, light and confident. Everin peeked around the edge of the wall.

Zale Nightwind.

Of course.

His silver hair glinted in the glow of the arc-lamps, and he walked like he owned the place. Beside him was Thorian Ashmore, full of swagger, followed by two final-year girls who might as well have been part of his fan club. One of them, of course, was Selene Veyra, glittering even in the dim light.

Everin ducked behind a pillar as the group came closer. Her heart gave a sharp twist. So he really had taken the bait. Their carefully staged conversation in the library had worked, and now Zale had come strutting down here to prove himself, to make that recording he had bragged about.

"I told you it would work," Zale was saying smugly. He held up a small glass vial filled with silvery-blue liquid. "This one came from the Shield I won at Moonlight Revels. Lumerial Essence that breaks through mid-level magical barriers. Watch."

Everin had to grab Phoenix's sleeve to stop her from charging forward to correct him. "Not 'I,' you moron," Phoenix hissed under her breath. "We won the Moonlight Revels dance competition."

Everin's breath caught. She crouched lower, watching through a gap in the stonework as Zale poured the shimmering liquid along the barrier's edge.

A ripple tore through the magical seals as if someone had dropped a pebble into water. One by one, the three barriers shivered, shimmered, and fell.

Zale stepped forward like a prince returning to a forgotten throne. "Behold," he declared to his gang, arms spread wide. "My great ancestor."

Everin's heart raced as they entered the cavern, still unnoticed by the final years.

And then she saw it.

Braskora. The Alpha Dragon.

His massive body sprawled across the stone like a slumbering mountain. Scales shimmered like polished emerald and obsidian, veined with deep shadow and a faint glimmer of magic. Even in stillness, he radiated an ancient power that made the cavern feel too small to contain him.

A long silence pressed down.

Then, with a sound like stone grinding against stone, one immense eyelid lifted. A volcanic orange eye cracked open, its glow flooding the chamber.

Zale froze mid-strut, his swagger faltering under that gaze. But almost instantly he fumbled for his composure, tugging his phone from his pocket and angling it for a triumphant selfie. "The heir has arrived," he muttered under his breath, flashing a grin that looked more nervous than proud.

Braskora's gaze narrowed. A low, grating rumble rolled from his chest. "Descendant?" His words struck like hammer blows, ancient and heavy. The dragon's nostrils flared, a single sniff pulling in Zale's scent. His eye sharpened with contempt. "So weak?"

Zale gave a nervous laugh, nearly choking on it. He stumbled upright, straightened his jacket, and puffed his chest as if to reclaim his pride. "Weak?" he repeated, incredulous, pointing to himself.

Braskora exhaled. Just a puff. But the force of it hurled Zale backward, tumbling him across the cavern floor in a graceless sprawl.

"You are… disappointing," the Alpha rumbled, his voice echoing like thunder through stone.

Everin clamped a hand over her mouth. The silence that followed was almost comical.

Thorian blinked. "Uh… say what now?"

Zale tried again to record with his cell phone. "Just one second, great ancestor, let me get the…"

The dragon's growl rolled through the cavern like an earthquake. The sound hit Zale's phone with a force that rattled the glass, the device slipping from his sweaty fingers. It clattered to the stone and skidded across the floor, screen cracking with a pathetic chirp of static.

The girls gasped. Thorian pinched the bridge of his nose.

"Leave," the dragon said simply.

And they did. Quickly. One of the girls yelped and bolted. Selene's glittering skirt snagged on a rock as she stumbled after the girl. Zale, his proud expression shattered and phone still sparking faintly on the ground, scrambled to grab it before running out with the rest.

Once their footsteps faded, Tariel stepped out into the open. Everin followed, her heart still pounding.

Braskora's eyes cracked open, and the cavern blazed with molten orange light. Even his breathing shook through the stone floor beneath Everin's boots, vibrating up into her chest until her ribs ached. For a fleeting heartbeat, she thought he might treat them the way he had Zale's group—dismiss them as beneath his notice. Relief loosened her chest. Maybe they'd walk away unscathed.

But then his gaze found her.

The shift was immediate. The air grew heavy, pressing against her lungs like molten iron. His pupils shrank into razor slits, and the sheer weight of his attention slammed into her with suffocating force. He wasn't looking at all of them. He was looking at her.

Everin's stomach twisted sharply, as if some invisible thread had tethered her to the dragon. The connection was unbearable, too close, too raw. Every part of her screamed to run, but her legs refused to obey. She stood frozen, caught in the stare of something ancient and furious.

"Do it now," Tariya hissed somewhere behind her.

Jackson moved with the vial, but Everin hardly saw him. Braskora's chest expanded, fire simmering in his throat, and dread sank into her bones. That fire wasn't meant for them. It was meant for her.

The roar that followed shattered the cavern walls. Heat seared her face as flame erupted in a torrent, the brightness blinding her. Everin stumbled backward, coughing, her vision smeared with smoke and ash.

"He's aiming for her!" Tariya cried.

Braskora's claws struck the ground beside her, stone exploding in jagged shards that cut across her arms. Panic tore through her as her sapphire shaft flared weakly in her grasp, forming a fragile barrier. The dragon fire slammed against it with brutal force, splintering the light and driving her to her knees. A broken sound escaped her throat, which was half sob, and half whimper.

"Everin!"

Tariel's voice cut through the chaos. He was suddenly in front of her, shaft raised, scattering the fire into a rain of sparks. Heat still licked at her skin, but he held back the worst of it.

Her thoughts spiraled. Why me? Why is he trying to kill me?

Around her, the battle blurred—Phoenix's shaft partially blazing, Tariya's strikes ringing against Braskora's armored hide, Jackson shouting orders. But Everin could barely focus. Every beat of the dragon's wings, every swing of his claws, every arc of fire, his every move was angled toward her.

Braskora lunged, his teeth snapping so close she felt the rush of air whip her hair against her face. She scrambled backward on hands and heels, terror clawing up her throat, until the cavern shook with the crash of his wing.

Through the chaos, she caught a glimpse of Jackson darting along the dragon's flank, vial clutched tight in his hand. He moved quickly, skirting falling debris, ducking beneath the sweep of Braskora's tail.

"Keep him busy!" he shouted.

Phoenix and Tariya surged forward with shafts raised, light flashing as they struck against Braskora's scales. While Tariel held the line in front of Everin, deflecting a jet of fire that split the air.

Then Jackson's voice rang out above the roar. "Got it!"

He held the vial high, its glass shimmering faintly with the dust inside. Relief flashed across Everin's chest, but Braskora's gaze swung back to her almost instantly, as though the collection hadn't mattered at all. His fury was still hers to bear.

The dragon's eyes never left her.

Flames built again in his throat, brighter and hotter. Her body was locked in place. She could do nothing but stare into that molten gaze, feel it tearing at her insides, searching for something she didn't understand.

Then Tariel spoke.

Not English. Not Dracos. Something older. The sound rolled through the air, deep and resonant, vibrating in Everin's chest like a memory she didn't own. Each syllable was heavy with power, lyrical, commanding, and undeniable.

Braskora froze. The fire guttered out mid-breath. Slowly, his gaze tore away from Everin and fixed on Tariel.

The shift was staggering. The Alpha's massive head lowered, bowing in deliberate deference.

"Ancient tongue," Braskora rumbled, voice like stone grinding against stone. "Spoken true… after centuries."

Everin's knees nearly buckled. She couldn't comprehend how

the same dragon who had moments ago tried to burn her alive was now lowering his head to Tariel. Was it surrendering to the spell that Tariel was casting, or was it showing respect to Tariel? Perhaps the former decided Everin as she was still shaken from the alpha dragon's attacks.

The cavern dimmed as Braskora's eye slid closed. Smoke coiled from his nostrils, and the crushing heat ebbed into silence.

Everin gasped, sucking in air like she hadn't been breathing. Her hands shook around the shaft, her palms slick with sweat. She was sure that the Braskora's fury had been meant for her.

And yet, he had obeyed Tariel.

"Run," Tariel said hoarsely.

She didn't argue. None of them did. They all fled as the protective layers of charm started to rise again.

Just as they rounded the bend near the upper access corridor, Everin froze.

Voices drifted down the hall. Zale's voice. He was still there. So much for thinking they'd gone far.

Everin slowed instinctively, catching the edges of Thorian's cocky laughter.

Before she could warn others, a shout echoed off the stone.

"Hey! Who's there?!"

"Go!" Tariel barked.

They split.

Jackson, Phoenix, and Tariya darted toward the upper dormitory routes. Their footsteps faded fast, cloaked by dark tunnels.

Tariel grabbed Everin's hand without warning, tugging her toward a side passage she hadn't even noticed.

"This way!"

"Where does it go?" she asked breathlessly.

"To the old observatory tower," he said. "Trust me."

She did.

They tore down the forgotten corridor, skimming past cracked murals and rusted pipes. At the far end stood a warped wooden door overgrown with ivy and half-crumbled charms. Tariel shoved it open, pulled her inside, and closed it behind them.

The air inside was still and cool, smelling faintly of dust and old stars.

Everin looked around in wonder. The space stretched up into a narrow, circular tower capped with a domed glass ceiling. Broken constellations flickered faintly in the magical panels above, part projection, part remnant of the old observatory's arcane design.

"This is the Astronomical Tower," she whispered. "I didn't even know it was still here."

"Most people don't," Tariel said. "Too close to the Headmaster's wing. Nobody wants to risk sneaking this far."

Everin let out a breathless laugh, brushing windblown strands of hair from her face. "And yet here we are."

Tariel looked at her, really looked, and in the aftermath of the dragon's cavern, the moonlight cast soft gold across his cheekbones, his collar, the rise and fall of his breath. His eyes were still dilated, bright and watchful.

Neither of them spoke.

They were still standing close to where he'd pulled her inside, his hand still hovering near hers, as if uncertain whether to let go.

"I can't believe we actually did it," she said softly. "We have all three ingredients now."

Tariel nodded. "Yeah. I wasn't sure we'd make it."

His voice was low, rough around the edges.

Everin stepped back, her shoulders brushing the curved stone. Tariel held still, the space between them shrinking to a heartbeat.

The glow of the old star map shimmered above them. Dust floated like stilled magic in the air.

"I, um…" she started, then forgot the rest of her sentence.

He leaned in slightly, almost unconsciously, like the gravity between them was playing its own magic of pull.

Their eyes met. His hand brushed her arm. He came closer and Everin forgot to breathe.

CHAPTER 20

The Kiss and the Footsteps

The moment hung between them like a breath suspended in starlight.

Tariel's gaze flicked down to her lips, and before Everin could think or second-guess or panic, he leaned in and kissed her.

It wasn't wild or desperate. Just a soft, unsure brush of his lips against hers. A question, not a claim.

Everin's breath caught. Her eyes fluttered shut, heart thudding against her ribs like it was trying to fly.

For a heartbeat, she leaned into him.

For a heartbeat, nothing else in the world existed, just the warmth of his mouth, the steady weight of his presence, and the faint scent of pine and spice that always seemed to cling to his jacket.

But then, she stepped back.

The moment snapped like a string pulled too tight.

Her fingers rose to her lips. "I… I have to go," she said, voice barely a whisper.

Tariel's brows lifted slightly, searching her expression, but he didn't move to stop her.

That's when they both heard it: footsteps, slow but approaching. Someone was walking past the tower's base, maybe even heading toward the stairwell.

Everin's heart tripped. "I have to go," she repeated, firmer this time.

She didn't look back.

She didn't dare.

Because if she did, she wasn't sure she'd have the strength to leave again.

She slipped out the narrow door, boots whispering against the stone as she hurried into the corridor.

The night air was cool beneath the covered walkway, lanterns burning low and throwing pale rings across the floor. Everin slowed when she spotted movement at the far end.

A small group of draggrels worked steadily, brushes in hand as they painted the walkway posts. It was easier to do such tasks at night, when students weren't underfoot. Pity stirred in Everin's chest. Did they ever rest? They always seemed to be working, day and night.

Professor Stark stood among them, tall and sharp in the dim light, her voice brisk as she gestured toward the posts. The draggrels grumbled but obeyed, their tails sweeping against the stone.

Everin ducked quickly behind one of the arching columns, pressing herself into the shadows. If Stark saw her wandering here at this hour, there would be questions, and she surely didn't want a confrontation with a professor at this hour of the night.

She held her breath as Stark's voice carried closer, then finally receded. A moment later, Stark and the draggrels turned down another path, their figures swallowed by the gloom.

Everin stayed still until the sound of their footsteps faded completely. Only then did she slip away into the night, her thoughts unsettled.

Had Stark seen what they were doing beneath the Academy? Did she know and simply chose not to interfere?

The questions lingered, heavy as stone, as Everin disappeared into the shadows.

The quiet creak of the dormitory door gave Everin away.

She slipped inside, her boots barely making a sound on the woven rug. Moonlight seeped through the tall windows, mingling with the dim glow of lanterns that lit the bunks and trunks. Inside, everything was warm, alive, and scented faintly of lavender warding charms.

Phoenix was sprawled across her bed in silk pajama shorts and a hoodie that sparkled faintly at the seams, legs dangling off the side as she scrolled through her phone.

Tariya sat cross-legged with a bowl of honey-dusted popcorn floating lazily in front of her, snatching kernels midair with well-practiced ease.

Both of them were giggling.

"I swear his scream echoed," Phoenix laughed. "It wasn't even a proper dragon growl, it was like a startled goat!"

"That wasn't a scream," Tariya argued, eyes twinkling. "That was a high-pitched Zale-is-about-to-get-scaled panic yelp."

"I wish I'd recorded it," Phoenix sighed dreamily. "I'd make it my ringtone."

Everin tried to slip past them unnoticed.

"Where have you been?" Tariya asked, not missing a beat. "You and Tariel just… vanished."

Everin tugged off her jacket and casually tossed it onto the foot of her bed. "We ran in the opposite direction. I didn't see anyone, so I came back."

Not a lie.

Not exactly the truth either.

"Mmhmm," Phoenix said, suspiciously. "Well, you didn't miss the premium comedy. Zale tried to puff out his chest like 'I'm the bloodline of Braskora,' and then the dragon practically sneezed, and they all bolted like squirrels in storm wind."

"Classic Nightwind confidence," Tariya muttered.

Everin smiled faintly but said nothing, busying herself with unlacing her boots.

Phoenix flopped back dramatically against her pillows. "But seriously, what was that language Tariel used?" she asked, glancing at Tariya. "Sounded like old draconian or something worse."

Tariya shook her head, her brows furrowed in thought. "It wasn't anything I've read. Maybe one of those deep dialects, ancient bonding tongues, maybe? Stuff even the Council lost centuries ago."

"But you can't deny the fact that Tariel excels in Draconian language," reasoned Phoenix.

Everin said nothing. She remembered the sound of Tariel's voice in the cavern, low and steady, like he wasn't reciting the words, he was remembering them.

Like they were buried inside him.

Like they'd always been there.

But that wasn't what was crowding her thoughts now.

It was the kiss.

Brief, gentle and unexpected.

Her lips still tingled where his had touched hers.

And she had pulled away.

Why? Why had she done that?

Heat flushed her cheeks as she stared down at her blankets, jaw clenched. It wasn't that she didn't want to. Heavens, she'd wanted to. But something about the suddenness, the spark between them, had scared her.

And now she didn't know what to do about it.

She barely heard the rest of the girls' conversation as it drifted into musings about what Braskora might have done if they hadn't escaped.

Everin lay down, rolled onto her side, and pulled the covers up to her chin.

But sleep wasn't coming.

Only the memory of the kiss.

And the heartbeat she hadn't been ready for.

The next day, Tariel stood just outside the Language of Dracos classroom, arms crossed and leaning casually against the stone archway. The hall was quiet, with only the occasional sound of boots echoing off the polished floors. Sunlight slanted through narrow windows, but his mind was fixed on one thing.

Everin.

He knew she'd seen him. The moment she turned the corner, her gaze locked on his, only for her eyes to immediately drop to the floor. Her steps slowed ever so slightly, enough for him to know she was thinking about last night.

Good, he thought, because he was too.

As she neared, Tariel pushed off the wall and blocked her path with a grin. Before she could utter a protest, he gently took her hand in his.

Everin gasped softly, twisting her wrist. "Tariel, what are you doing?" she whispered, glancing nervously down the hall. "Let go!"

He just tightened his grasp so she couldn't break free, not that she was trying hard. "Not until you stop pretending last night didn't happen," he whispered back. "You ran off like a thief."

Her cheeks flushed. "I didn't run off."

Tariel arched a brow. "You bolted."

Before she could answer, a familiar voice interrupted.

"Hold up, are you two dating now?" Phoenix Bevington's voice rang out behind them, a smirk riding her lips. "Or is this some secret handshake situation I wasn't briefed on?"

Jackson strolled in behind her, grinning. "About time, if you ask me."

Everin nearly leapt away from Tariel. "It's not what you think."

"We're not dating," Tariel said, then added with a teasing glance at Everin, "Yet."

Phoenix burst into laughter. "Well, finally some entertainment in this special language class for the four of us only."

Inside the sleek, arc-shaped classroom, the four took their

usual seats, Phoenix and Jackson near the middle, Tariel and Everin at the back. The front wall was mounted with a smart-board, glowing softly in the dim light. Above them, floating parchment rolls hovered quietly, occasionally flipping with a papery flutter. Though it was modern, the Academy also had dragon magic in every corner.

Tariel pulled his chair closer to Everin, just enough for his shoulder to almost brush hers. She looked stiff. Guarded.

He leaned slightly, murmuring, "Meet me after the classes in the Observatory."

Her eyes shot to his. "Why?"

"So we can finish what we started yesterday."

"What?" Everin looked horrified.

Tariel smiled. "The elixir, or do you want to sit with Professor Vantle and use his cauldron in the Potions Lab?"

She muttered something under her breath about arrogant dragon-boys and stared straight ahead.

Tariel almost grinned.

Almost.

He hadn't missed the way her breath caught when he touched her. Or the way her hand had lingered, just for a second, before she pulled away. She felt it too. Whatever it was.

But he couldn't dwell.

Associate lecturer, Mrs. Inkpen strode in with that signature brisk grace, her robes crisp and her hair twisted into a severe knot. Her scarf, dark emerald and embroidered with curling charms, trailed behind her like a tame serpent.

"Good morning," she said, eyes sweeping across them. "Today, we begin working with the Draco Letter Boxes. You'll practice summoning symbols and focusing magical control without physical contact. Once you can do this, saying the sounds, reading words, and understanding them would come naturally to you."

She waved her hand, and four carved boxes floated from her desk to theirs. Each one was etched with clawed glyphs and shimmered with an inner pulse, like something breathing quietly inside.

Tariel's box landed with a soft thud. These boxes were ancient tools infused with trace amounts of Alpha Dragon magic.

Enough to awaken the language instinct in dragon-blooded students. Enough to test who was paying attention.

From the corner of his eye, Tariel watched Everin.

She blinked down at her box, brow creased in awe. Her fingers hovered over the lid, tentative, like she wasn't sure whether to open a gift or a curse. When she finally unclasped it, Tariel saw the black mist swirl and form silver symbols, alive, shifting, beautiful.

She inhaled sharply, wonder plain on her face.

He smiled to himself.

She always looked at the world like it was half miracle, half mystery. No matter how tired, no matter how suspicious of his smirks, she had that spark. He liked that about her.

"All right," Inkpen said. "Boxes open. Try to guide the symbols with your focus. Do not touch them. Channel through your inner link."

Tariel opened his own. The mist curled obediently, symbols rising like dancers in response to his thoughts.

Then Phoenix's voice cut through the concentration.

"Mrs. Inkpen," she said, batting her lashes, "before we start, last night, Tariel said something in a language none of us recognized. It wasn't on the translation sheets. Any chance we could talk about rare Draconian tongues today?"

Tariel's hand froze above his letters.

Inkpen arched a brow and turned to him. "Mr. Fenwick, would you indulge us? Recite the phrase. Let's see what you've been dabbling in."

Tariel's stomach clenched.

He hadn't expected this. Not now. Not so soon.

He'd spent half the night scouring the language archives in the restricted section. Runes, dialects, even lost tongues from the Southern Wastes. Nothing matched what he had said. The syllables had come from somewhere deep inside him, instinct, maybe. Memory. Or something older.

The words had come unbidden, ancient and primal, spoken from something buried deep in his bones. It hadn't sounded like any language he'd studied, Dracos, Valmerian, or even Rune-Script. It had just… come to him.

But he couldn't tell them that.

He cleared his throat, keeping his voice steady. "It was… just something old. From a dead dialect. I think it was called Vernasharic."

Inkpen's eyes lit up. "Ah, yes. Vernasharic. Ancient trade tongue from the East Skyholds. You're right, very few speak it now. Well done, Tariel. Rare knowledge, indeed."

He nodded once, forcing himself to stay calm.

But beneath the desk, his fingers curled into fists.

He hated lying. But he hated attention even more.

Not after the Severance Spell. Not after the glow of bonding magic during the Moonlight Revels. And definitely not after the strange, fire-slicked vision of Braskora watching him like he was a threat. He knew others felt that Braskora was lashing out at Everin, but he was right behind her. He wasn't sure whether it was Everin or him that Braskora was attacking.

He could still hear his mother's voice in his mind from days ago: "Do you think he… he's… the feared one the Council is whispering about?"

Tariel didn't want to be the one. He just wanted to figure out what was happening to him before the rest of the world did.

He could feel the eyes on him now, Phoenix's curious gaze, Jackson's skeptical brow raise, even Everin's sidelong glance, half worried, half knowing.

And he knew.

They didn't fully believe him.

He stared down at his box, watching the Draco runes spiral into a perfect ring above his palm.

He didn't even believe himself.

CHAPTER 21

The Elixir Begins

The spiral staircase creaked beneath Everin's boots as she climbed toward the top of the Astronomy Tower. Moonlight filtered through the narrow windows, striping the stone walls with silver bands. Her breath fogged in the chill air, and she tucked a strand of hair behind her ear as she reached the landing.

When she stepped inside the tower, the sight made her pause. Tariel was already there, alone, focused, radiant in the soft glow of lanternlight. A cauldron sat in the center of a long table, surrounded by vials and scrolls. An old parchment was spread out before him, pinned by glass bottles containing rare herbs and glimmering powders. His dark hair fell slightly over his brow as he leaned forward, reading.

Everin's heart gave a traitorous thump.

He looked up. Their eyes locked. Something slow and electric passed between them.

"You're early," Tariel said, his voice lower than usual. Warm. But there was a weight behind it she couldn't quite read.

Everin tried not to fidget. She knew she was guilty.

He had asked her to come in the afternoon.

Now it was well past dinner, the sky a deep indigo outside the tower windows. And he hadn't even come down to the dining hall. Was he upset with her?

Before she could ask, the sound of approaching footsteps broke the moment. Jackson, Phoenix, and Tariya entered the observatory with a quiet flurry of coats and whispers.

"Wow," Jackson said, glancing around. "Perfect hideout. Creepy, remote, vaguely haunted. Love it."

Tariel gave him a nod and walked over to a small metal box etched with swirling sigils. "This'll cast an illusion on the doorway," he explained. "To anyone passing by, it'll look like a dusty, abandoned tower. Broken furniture. Nothing of inter-est."

Everin stepped forward and set her satchel down next to a

bundle of thin twigs and root clippings. "You think that charm will keep people away?"

Tariel nodded once. "Most people. But we need to activate it." He turned to Tariya. "It needs a dragon's breath to work."

Tariya sighed. "Of course it does." She crossed her arms and gave Jackson a mock glare. "I'm the only one here who can fully transform without blowing holes in the ceiling."

Jackson raised both hands in mock surrender. "Hey, I'd help, but you don't want me setting fire to this place. Still working on aim and control, remember?"

Tariya rolled her eyes. "Exactly."

"Please," Phoenix muttered, smirking. "My dragon will sparkle the whole tower."

"When? In the next decade, when it finally decides to appear?" Jackson teased.

"And why exactly are we making this Igniflorum Primus elixir?" Phoenix gave her best duh look to Jackson.

In a fluid motion, Tariya shifted, her form elongating, eyes gleaming. Wings shimmered into being, and scales rippled across her arms. Her dragon form emerged quickly, compact and beautiful in the golden torchlight. She blew a steady stream of warm breath across the box.

The carvings lit up, spinning into motion.

A subtle ripple shimmered through the air as a magical veil fell across the room. The doorway flickered, then dimmed. Anyone on the outside would now see only cobwebs and ruin.

Tariel handed Everin a smooth dragon scale. "Keep this with you. It'll let you see through the illusion."

"There are only two," Everin noted.

He gave a small shrug. "One for me. One for you."

Everin's heart did that odd flutter again. She quickly tucked the scale into her pocket.

They gathered around the table. Phoenix unrolled the old parchment showing the process. Ink scrawls illustrated each step of the elixir's brewing, a rare combination of ancient in-gredients and precision.

"The Veilvine sap, Emberroot, and Alpha dragon dust," Tariel said, laying each vial out carefully. "We combine them first, then add the flux agent and catalyst root. Then it simmers, rests, is strained, cooled, and distilled."

Tariya frowned. "How long does all that take?"

"A week," Everin replied, reading the parchment upside down.

Phoenix groaned. "This better give us superpowers."

They got to work. Hours passed in a haze of measuring, pouring, whispering, and stirring. The cauldron's contents shifted from burnt gold to deep rose as the mixture thickened. Light steam curled into the air like dragon breath.

At last, Tariel straightened, stretching his arms. "Alright. Time to seal it and let it rest."

The three others gathered their things. As they neared the door, Tariel touched Everin's shoulder gently.

"Can you stay a moment?" he whispered.

Her heart jumped.

She nodded slowly. "I'll help tidy up and follow," she added, trying to sound casual.

Phoenix smirked as she paused at the door. "Just say you need alone time, Haydon. We'll leave you to it."

Tariya gave Everin a wide-eyed look. "Wait. What's happening?"

"I'll brief you later," Phoenix whispered with a grin, tugging Tariya along.

Jackson raised a brow but said nothing. The three vanished through the doorway, the magical veil falling behind them.

Everin turned to face Tariel in the suddenly quiet tower. Her palms tingled.

"What is it?" she asked softly, feeling her pulse drum in her ears.

"You made me wait," Tariel said, stepping closer. "You didn't come this afternoon."

"I never said I would," Everin replied, backing up slightly. Her voice betrayed more nerves than she wanted.

"You knew I was waiting."

She shrugged, tilting her chin up, trying to seem unaffected.

"So?"

Tariel closed the distance, towering over her. Damn, she couldn't think straight when he came close.

Everin lowered her eyes. She couldn't hold his intense gaze, especially when she was lying. She had wanted to come running after the lectures, but she had decided to give herself some time to be sure.

Slowly, Tariel lifted her chin, making her look at him, drawn to his brown eyes. Then he lowered his lips and claimed hers. It wasn't a mere brush this time, but a light, gentle, and testing kiss.

Her breath hitched. Her eyes fluttered closed.

He stopped and looked at her, reading her warm face.

Then his mouth returned to hers, surer now, more eager. Her fingers curled into his jacket as she returned his kisses. They moved back toward the table, his arms around her, her heart soaring and stumbling all at once. Glass vials clinked as her hip nudged the edge.

The kiss broke, as both of them became breathless.

Tariel smiled, eyes glinting.

"I like you, Everin," he said simply. "I want to date you."

Her cheeks flushed crimson. "You really don't believe in subtlety, do you?"

"Nope."

She gave a small, shy nod. "Okay."

Tariel grinned. "Okay?"

Everin grinned back. "Okay."

The days passed like a blur, but the evenings belonged to them.

Each night, after dinner and Academy duties, Everin found herself quietly slipping away from her dormitory, heart beating faster than it should, fingers tightening around her satchel. By now, she knew the creaky stair near the library tower to avoid, the exact pace to walk so her footsteps wouldn't echo in the stone corridors.

And waiting for her, always already there, was Tariel.

The Observatory had become their secret world. The hidden cauldron shimmered beneath layers of illusion charms, the potion slowly evolving from its dusky, thick beginning into something silken, radiant, and faintly glowing. The Igniflorum Primus elixir. A miracle in the making.

But what Everin treasured more than the magical process was everything that happened around it.

Their conversations were often simple, sometimes deep.

One night, while stirring the elixir gently with a golden-glass rod, Tariel leaned back on his elbows and said, "What if we never transform?"

Everin blinked. She hadn't expected that.

"I mean…" he glanced sideways at her. "We're both late bloomers. You, me, even Phoenix. Jackson's started shifting. Tariya's practically majestic. What if this part of us never wakes up?"

Everin tapped the edge of the glass vial. "I think… there's more to us than shifting into a dragon. You've already done things most wouldn't dream of. The Severance Spell. The bonding glow. Whatever that was with Braskora."

Tariel smiled, eyes searching her face. "You are right, but most of those were unexpected."

She looked away, flushed. "But it has, and we just need to figure out how it happened."

That earned her a soft laugh, one that curled warm in her chest.

Some nights, they talked for hours. About childhood memories. About favorite books and family. One evening, as Everin set her bag down, her cell phone buzzed. She stepped aside to answer, while Tariel busied himself with the cauldron.

"Everin?" Samuel's voice cracked through the line. "I'm so tired. There's no food. Nobody cares. I miss you."

Her chest ached. She soothed him gently, urging him to stay strong until she returned. When the call ended, another came through. Beth.

Her mother's voice was thick, words slurred. "Stop filling Samuel's head with things you don't understand, Everin. Don't forget, I'm the mum, not you."

Everin's throat burned. "I know I'm not the mum. But I've been looking after him like one. If you were responsible, I wouldn't have to. For once, forget the pain of being married to a man who won't be there. Move on, mum. You have your children. They need you."

A scoff. Then the line went dead.

She set the phone facedown, her fingers trembling.

Tariel came quietly and sat beside her. He didn't press. He didn't question. At last, she said, "She hates him for never being there. But he works in the mines. They don't let workers leave. He couldn't stay even if he wanted. He belongs to the dragon world, not the non-Draco one."

Tariel's gaze was steady. "That isn't your burden. They are adults. You are not at fault. Sometimes people learn the hard way. That doesn't make it yours to carry."

Her eyes stung, but she managed a small smile. He hadn't judged. He hadn't tried to fix it. Just stayed close, steady as the glow in the cauldron.

Other nights, they sat in silence, his thigh brushing hers as they watched the potion swirl, or passed notes scribbled with doodles and inside jokes. Everin felt like the universe had slowed down, wrapping them both in a bubble of warm golden light that only they could see.

And after each night, when she finally returned to her dorm, often well past curfew, sneaking back with whispered spells of silence, her phone would buzz softly under her pillow.

Tariel: Still thinking about your laugh.
Tariel: That potion isn't the only magic we're making.
Tariel: Can't wait to see you tomorrow.

She would smile like a fool in the dark, type something back, usually teasing, sometimes sincere, and then drift off to sleep with her fingers still curled around the phone.

A week passed like that.

A week of secrets, starlight, brewing elixirs, and building something between them that felt bigger than either of them could name.

And when the potion was finally ready, softly glowing in its completed form, stable and ready to be bottled, Everin knew.

This was more than magic.

CHAPTER 22

Fire in the Blood

Everin stood near the Observatory table, staring at the three completed vials of Igniflorum Primus in crystalline glass, sealed with arcane wax, each vial glowing with a pulsing golden hue like bottled starlight.

"We really did it," Phoenix whispered, her voice barely above the rustle of the night wind against the tower's glass panels. "That actually looks like magic."

Jackson gave a low whistle. "I thought it'd be more… smoky. Or bubbling. This looks like dragon champagne."

Tariya rolled her eyes but smiled. "That's because you didn't help stir. Or distill. Or stay up past midnight, measuring the temperature. This," she said, gesturing to the vials, "is a miracle."

Three vials.

Everin's stomach turned, but not from nerves. More like the weight of possibility. Or hope.

Tariel stepped forward and picked up one vial, examining it under the moonlight. "Cheers to the ones who haven't shifted yet."

His gaze swept to Everin and Phoenix. Then quietly, he handed each of them a vial.

Everin held her vial in both hands, heart racing. "So… we just drink it?"

Tariel gave a crooked grin. "Unless you'd like to try rubbing it on your forehead first."

Phoenix shot him a glare. "Don't tempt me."

Jackson raised a brow. "What if you all burst into scales right now? Do I get to say I told you so?"

Everin popped the seal on her vial. It gave a tiny click, like a lock unlatching in the air. She took a breath, glanced once at Tariel, then tipped the potion back.

It was warm. Not scalding, but rich like swallowing sunlight.

Tariel and Phoenix drank theirs in unison, all three of them watching each other with hesitant anticipation.

A beat of silence passed.

Then another.

Everin looked at her hands. Nothing.

Phoenix blinked. "Should we be glowing?"

"I don't feel any different," Tariel said, frowning slightly. "You?"

"Nope," Everin muttered.

"Maybe it takes time," Jackson offered.

"Maybe we brewed magical tea," Phoenix added, sticking her tongue out. "Very fancy tea."

They laughed, all of them, the tension evaporating for the moment.

The vials were set aside, empty and still warm to the touch.

"Alright," Tariya yawned, stretching her arms. "I vote we sleep and see what happens tomorrow. If I hear dragon roars in the hallway, I'll know someone got lucky."

"Deal," Tariel said, giving Everin's hand a brief squeeze before letting go. "See you all in the morning."

They all began packing up quietly, slipping through the enchanted wards and into the quiet corridors of Drakon Academy.

Everin's steps were slow. She kept glancing down at her hands, half-expecting to see sparks or shimmering scales.

But nothing came.

Still, something stirred in her chest like a slow, quiet hum as if something was waiting.

Waiting to wake.

Later that night, the dormitory was quiet, save for the occasional creak of old wood or a faint breeze brushing against the windowpanes.

Everin lay curled beneath her blankets, the warmth of the covers doing little to soothe the unease growing in her chest. Her thoughts spun in circles about potions, dragon blood, Tariel's hand in hers, and the elixir she had taken.

Eventually, sleep claimed her.

She stood in a forest of ash.

The trees were skeletal, blackened trunks that reached like claws toward a colorless sky. Fire flickered in the distance, silent but hungry, devouring everything it touched without sound or smoke.

Then she heard it.

Wings.

Massive. Slow. Heavy as thunderclouds.

Everin turned, and the world shifted.

Before her stood a dragon, twice the size of anything she had imagined. Its scales were dark as obsidian, but in the shadows they rippled with subtle green undertones, like molten veins beneath stone. The beast's eyes blazed into a vivid, unnatural green, not glowing, but burning. Alive with purpose.

It stared at her.

Not just at her, but through her.

Into her.

"Everin."

Her name echoed like a drumbeat. Not spoken aloud, but planted deep within her bones.

She staggered back.

"Who… who are you?" she tried to say, but her voice cracked and vanished before it reached the air.

The dragon stepped forward.

With every slow, deliberate movement, the forest crumbled into flame. The world darkened. The heat rose.

It opened its mouth, and for a terrifying moment, Everin thought it would breathe fire.

But instead, it smiled.

"Come find me."

Everin sat bolt upright in bed.

Her breath tore from her throat like she'd been drowning. Her sheets were soaked. Her heart pounded like war drums.

Moonlight poured through the window. Her roommate, Phoenix, snored softly in the other bed, blissfully unaware.

Everin placed a hand on her chest.

The hum from earlier, when she drank the elixir, was back.

Louder now.

Alive.

And beneath that hum, something darker was calling.

She whispered to the empty room, "What's happening to me?"

But no answer came.

CHAPTER 23

The Voice in the Dark

Tariel jolted in bed, tangled in damp sheets. Sweat clung to his brow, his shirt plastered to his back. His breath came in uneven gasps, chest rising and falling like he'd just sprinted up the North Tower stairs.

A dim light filtered through the curtains of his bedroom. It was early morning.

He sat up, his fingers digging into the mattress. The dream was already slipping from him like smoke—shapeless, colorless. Only the sense of it remained.

"Good, you're awake," Jackson muttered, perched at the edge of the bed. "You were freaking me out, man."

Tariel rubbed his face, spotting Jackson nearby. The sight made him realize they were in his dad's quarters, where Jackson had come for a sleepover. "What happened?" he asked.

"You were muttering. Loud. Some ancient-sounding dragon tongue I couldn't place."

Tariel stilled. "You understood any of it?"

"Nope," Jackson said. "But I recorded it."

He held up his phone and hit play.

Tariel listened in silence. The voice on the recording was definitely his, but it was low, rhythmic, and laced with power. The syllables were unfamiliar, raw. Nothing they'd studied. Not in any textbook. Not in any known dialect.

But he understood them.

Darkness is coming.

It chilled him more than the dream he couldn't remember. Jackson waited, eyebrows raised.

Tariel forced a chuckle and waved it off. "Relax. That's Old Vathrien. A rare dialect from the northern Spire colonies. I came across it during some independent reading."

Jackson blinked. "That's... a thing?"

Tariel nodded. "Yeah. It means something like 'Fire walks with caution.' I'm paraphrasing. You know I like picking up weird linguistic scraps."

Jackson stared at him for a beat, then shrugged. "Well, remind me not to be near your creepy dreams."

As Jackson padded back to his makeshift bed, Tariel sank into the mattress, jaw tight.

He had lied.

Because what he said wasn't Vathrien. It wasn't anything recorded.

No one knew this language.

And yet, somehow, he did.

He stared into the dark, the echo of his voice still ringing in his ears.

Darkness is coming.

The clatter of cutlery and the scent of cinnamon toast filled the Drakon Academy dining hall. Morning sunlight spilled through the high arched windows, casting golden light over tables lined with students.

Tariel spotted them first. Everin, Phoenix, Tariya, and Jackson were gathered at their usual spot near the back corner. A place just quiet enough to feel like it was theirs.

He slid into the seat beside Everin, nudging her with his elbow. She gave him a quick smile that didn't quite meet her eyes.

"So?" Phoenix asked, practically bouncing in her seat. "Did anyone, I don't know... combust? Grow wings overnight? Breathe fire in their sleep?"

Tariya rolled her eyes. "Can we have one breakfast without the dramatics?"

"I'm just saying," Phoenix said, lowering her voice and leaning in, "we drank a mythical elixir last night. Something magical should've happened."

All eyes turned to Tariel, Everin, and Phoenix, the three who'd taken the elixir.

Tariel lifted his coffee mug and shrugged. "Nothing. Not yet."

"Same here," Everin said quickly, but her glance flicked to Tariel and lingered. A question passed silently between them. A flicker of doubt. Or memory.

"Ugh," Phoenix muttered, stabbing her fruit with a fork. "I was hoping for wings at the very least."

"You didn't get anything?" Tariya asked.

"Nothing," Phoenix grumbled. "Unless fashion sense counts as transformation."

Tariel set his mug down, voice lower now. "You realize it was hidden in the Restricted Section for a reason. Maybe it wasn't meant to be brewed... maybe it doesn't even work."

Everin hesitated, her spoon halfway to her mouth. "Or worse," she said softly, "maybe it has side effects we don't know about yet."

The table went quiet for a beat, the unspoken weight of the thought pressing over them.

Then Phoenix tossed her braid back with a huff. "Well, if my side effect is looking fabulous, I'll take it."

Jackson took a bite of toast and said through a mouthful,

"Well, Tariel didn't shift or get a fabulous lip job, but he did say something weird last night. Like creepy weird. Mumbled some ancient-sounding nonsense in his sleep."

Phoenix turned sharply. "What kind of nonsense?"

Jackson shrugged. "Sounded like a spell. Or a prophecy. Or like… Vathrien. Isn't that what it's called, Tariel?"

Tariel gave a tight smile. "Vathrien. Yeah. Old dialect. North coast region. Probably picked it up from one of the books I was reading."

Jackson narrowed his eyes. "Sounded darker than that."

"I like languages," Tariel said simply, sipping his tea. "Sometimes things just come out."

Everin gave him a look. Not accusing. Just curious.

He didn't meet her eyes.

Before anyone could ask more, the academy bell chimed overhead.

"Shapeshifting with Stark," Tariya groaned. "Better stretch your backs, kids."

They scraped their chairs back and filed out of the dining hall, heading toward the open training fields near the edge of the school's inner walls.

Tariel lingered just a moment behind the others. He glanced back at the table. At the untouched toast. At the words he'd spoken in a dream.

He had known exactly what they meant.

And the silence that followed them now was starting to feel heavier than it should.

The shapeshifting grounds were abuzz with energy as Professor Stark strode to the front of the circular training platform, her boots crunching against the enchanted gravel that shimmered faintly beneath their feet. Sunlight washed down from the wide sky above, casting shifting patterns of gold across the students who had begun to gather in small, whispering groups.

Usually, their lessons took place in the vast indoor hall of the east wing, but today, Stark had brought them outdoors into the open-air training grounds. "Fresh air strengthens focus," she had said briskly. "And I need room in case someone breathes fire."

Everin stood between Tariel and Phoenix, her heart a taut string strumming under her ribs. Her palms felt damp. She wasn't sure if it was nerves or anticipation.

"All right," Professor Stark called, folding her arms behind her back. "You know the drill. Ground yourself, focus, and draw your dragon energy forward. Controlled shaping only. No flare-ups or theatrics, unless you want to be cleaning dragon soot out of your ears until graduation."

A few students laughed.

Everin exhaled and lowered her gaze. She could see Tariya ahead, already crackling with warmth. A soft ripple coursed over her skin, and in a heartbeat, her dragon form broke through, revealing sleek silver scales, a long twisting tail, and wings that shimmered with lunar brilliance.

Gasps echoed as Tariya soared for a moment before gracefully landing, shifting back to human form with a proud grin.

"Show off," Phoenix muttered beside Everin.

"Jealous?" Jackson teased.

"Terribly."

Everin's eyes drifted to Tariel. His brows were drawn tight in concentration, jaw clenched. But nothing happened. Not even a flicker of scale. Phoenix, too, only managed a light warmth along her palms before it fizzled away.

They were still late bloomers like her.

"Miss Everin," Professor Stark's voice rang out.

Everin's breath caught.

She stepped forward onto the platform. The gravel beneath her boots seemed to pulse. Some students who could easily transform circled around the edges, eyes on her. Watching. Waiting.

Focus, just like before. Feel the magic. Pull it through.

She shut her eyes and listened.

At first, there was only silence.

Then something stirred.

It wasn't warm, like the others described. It was fiery, hot molten fire. It slid through her veins like molten lava. Her breath hitched. Her spine arched.

Then her eyes flew open, glowing bright, unnatural green.

She gasped.

Scales began to ripple across her arms, which were obsidian black and glistening like polished stone. Her fingernails sharpened into claws, her legs buckled, and smoke hissed from the corners of her mouth.

She had only transformed partially, but defying the laws of nature, a shadow appeared beneath her. Her shadow.

Dark as a moonless night, the shadow split into three large heads.

The watching students gasped as more joined in. Everin touched her partially scaled face. There was only one head, but why was the shadow showing three heads instead?

There was no time to think when her transformation was overtaking her senses.

Her body surged forward with a strength she'd never felt. Overwhelming power crashed through her chest. Her hair whipped around her face as wind gathered around her like a storm rising from the inside.

She wasn't scared.

She felt magnificent. Limitless. Eternal.

Like she could command oceans and set fire to the stars.

More gasps erupted.

"She's glowing. Look at her arms!"

"Unbelievable! The shadows don't match."

"And it's a three-headed dragon."

"Is that even possible?"

"Those aren't normal scales. Look at the shape…"

"Wait… are those Hell's Fire markings?"

"Is she…?"

Then one voice cut through the growing panic.

"She's the unique and most dangerous, the Hell's Fire dragon!"

"She's the Feared One!"

Screams followed. A few students backed away. Someone tripped. Another dropped their staff.

Everin's vision blurred. The green glow in her eyes sharpened to searing light. For a moment, it felt like the dragon inside her was laughing.

Triumphant.

Then it was gone.

Her knees gave out. She fell forward.

A hand caught her. It was Tariel's strong, assuring arm about her, and his eyes were full of concern.

Professor Stark's voice boomed, silencing the chaos.
"Enough!"

Everyone froze.

Everin slumped in Tariel's grip, her heart still pounding,

smoke curling from her lips. She looked up at him. His face was pale and alarmed.

"You okay?" he asked, his voice low.

"I… I don't know."

Professor Stark marched toward them, eyes narrowed, her expression dark and unreadable.

The silence that followed was deafening. Every eye was on her.

Everyone had seen it.

There was no denying it now.

Everin was the Hell's Fire Dragon and whatever that meant… the world was about to change.

Her chest tightened. The air felt too close, too heavy. Whispers pressed in from all directions, rising like a tide she couldn't escape. She pulled away from Tariel's steadying hand, shaking her head.

Not here. Not in front of them all.

Without another word, she turned and bolted. Past the gawking students, past the watchful gaze of Stark, through the stone archways that framed the courtyard. Her boots pounded the gravel, then the packed earth as the academy grounds gave way to the dark line of trees.

She didn't stop. Or rather, she couldn't stop until the forest swallowed her whole.

Everin ran until her lungs burned. The trees blurred around her, branches clawing at her sleeves, roots catching at her boots. She didn't stop until the academy's stone walls were swallowed behind her, until she reached the forest's edge where the shadows were thick and the air smelled of pine and damp earth.

She pressed her palms against a tree trunk, nails digging into the bark. Her breath came fast, ragged. Rage bubbled under her skin, too wild to contain. She tore at the moss with her boots, kicked loose stones into the dark. Her hands shook as she whispered to herself, over and over, "No. I'm still me. I won't let this thing control me. Not now, not ever."

Several lengthy minutes later, the fight drained out of her all at once. She slumped down at the base of the tree, knees pulled tight to her chest. Sobs came quietly, muffled into her sleeves. For a while, she let them come.

Then, slowly, the sobs faded. Her breath steadied. She raised her head, her cheeks damp but her jaw set. "I can do this," she murmured into the quiet. "I will do this. I'll show them I'm not what they think I am. I'll prove it."

A low hum drifted through the trees. Everin stilled, tilting her head. Beyond the canopy, faint streaks of light cut through the sky. They were choppers. Sleek, rune-bound, crest-marked. The Dragon Council. They were already here.

Her heart lurched, but she stayed rooted, watching the lights vanish beyond the treetops toward the academy. So it begins, she thought.

The lunch bell tolled, clear and distant. Everin brushed the tears from her face and pushed herself to her feet. Whatever waited inside, whispers or stares or worse, she would face it head-on.

And she walked back toward the hall.

CHAPTER 24

Whispers and Decisions

The dining hall buzzed with noise, but for Everin, it may as well have been silent.

It was lunchtime, but the moment she entered, it felt like the world shifted. Forks paused midair. Conversations fell to whispers. Her steps echoed louder than they should have across the marble floor. After randomly picking a few pieces of food, she slid into an empty seat at the end of one of the long wooden tables, head bowed, eyes fixed on her barely touched plate. It might as well have been a prison tray.

The whispers returned. Again.

"She's the Hell's Fire dragon."

"The Feared One..."

"She transformed, barely, and still the air burned."

Everin gritted her teeth and kept her gaze on her food, even though her appetite had vanished the moment she'd stepped inside. The worst part wasn't the fear. It was the distance. The way people, her classmates, even teachers, looked at her now. Like she was already becoming something terrible.

Out of the corner of her eye, she saw a familiar figure approaching. Then another. And another. Phoenix. Jackson. Tariya. And finally, Tariel.

They took the seats around her without saying a word at first. Just their presence made something loosen in Everin's chest.

Phoenix gave her a sly smirk as she sat down across from her. "You look like you could use a distraction."

"From what? The entire Academy's whispering behind my back?" Everin muttered, picking up her spoon and twirling it between her fingers.

"Ignore them," Tariya said, arms folded and gaze fierce. "They'll forget it in a week. Or move on to the next person to gossip about."

Jackson nodded. "Yeah, like maybe Zale's dating details. That'll give them enough to talk about for months."

That earned a small smile from Everin.

Phoenix leaned in, her voice low but curious. "But seriously… what do you think they're going to do? The Council's been alerted. Rumor is they're already on their way."

Everin swallowed hard, her fingers tightening around her spoon.

Tariel, who had been mostly quiet, finally spoke. "They're going to assess the situation." His voice was calm, but distant. "They won't act immediately."

"Yeah, 'assess,'" Jackson said. "That's usually Council-speak for 'panic dramatically then sentence someone.'"

Phoenix arched a brow. "Do you think they'd really… you know… come after Everin?"

The silence that followed stretched a little too long.

"I don't know," Tariel said eventually, pushing his tray aside. "But I need to go and meditate."

Everin glanced up, heart tugging. He hadn't even touched his food. He hadn't really looked at her. She wanted to stop him, ask what he was thinking, what he was feeling, but the words didn't come fast enough. He was already gone.

Phoenix nudged her foot under the table. "He's just trying to figure himself out, too."

"I know," Everin said softly, trying not to sound disappointed.

Across the dining hall, loud laughter broke out. Lizzy, the blonde final-year student who trailed after Zale like a shadow, was holding court at her table, speaking just loudly enough to be overheard.

"I heard she's a Hell's Fire dragon," Lizzy said, mockingly wide-eyed. "Bet she'll torch the whole Academy before she graduates."

Selene giggled. "Maybe we should switch dorms before she explodes."

Everin felt her cheeks burn, but Phoenix narrowed her eyes.

"Keep talking, Lizzy," she said loudly. "You'll make a great dragon snack if you keep it up."

Tariya chuckled, clearly unbothered. "I'd pay to see that."

Everin gave a tight smile, but deep down, she still felt that cold weight in her stomach.

The meditation chamber was quiet as stone. Only the faint glow of the rune-candles lit the carved walls, shadows pooling in the corners like secrets that had been waiting for centuries. Tariel sat cross-legged at first, trying to breathe the way the masters taught, steady and even. But the whispers from the dining hall clung to him.

Hell's Fire dragon. The Feared One. The curse reborn.

He dragged both hands through his hair and let out a frustrated groan. "I don't care," he muttered under his breath. "I don't care if she is the Hell's Fire dragon."

But he did. Not because he feared her. Because the truth gnawed at him.

All this time, listening to his parents' hushed arguments, their worried looks, the way they whispered that maybe he was the Feared One, he had almost believed it. Almost braced himself for the day someone would point a finger and call him cursed. And now? Relief washed through him, sharp and guilty. It wasn't him.

But the curse hadn't vanished. It had landed on Everin. The girl he…

He bit down hard on his lip. The girl he loved.

His chest tightened. What kind of cruel twist was this? The thing dragons feared most was buried inside the person who meant the most to him.

His mind drifted unwillingly back to the first time he saw her, not here, but several months ago, at college. She had been quiet, small in her presence, sitting alone on the bench with her nose in a book. He'd noticed how she'd sneak glances toward the basketball court, cheeks flushed when she thought no one was looking. But she wasn't looking at him. Her gaze always followed Jackson, the golden one, the one everyone admired. Tariel had laughed it off, told himself it didn't matter. And yet, when he saw her again at Drakon Academy, the spark had flared bright inside him.

He had rushed to her aid, yes, but beneath that was the selfish hope—maybe now she would see him. Maybe now those shy looks would be for him. He had gone out of his way to be near her, to be her friend, to weave his way into her circle, just to have a chance.

And now… now she carried a cursed soul. A soul said to belong to the demon lord Tynan.

His breath hitched. His hand curled into a fist on his knee. "How do I fight that?" he whispered harshly to the silence. "How do I protect her from something living inside her? From something even dragons fear?"

The words scraped his throat. He hated himself for how silent he'd been in the dining hall, how he hadn't stood up for her the way he should have. He cursed under his breath. Coward. Jerk. He told himself he had needed to think, to breathe before speaking, but the excuse sounded hollow.

He pushed himself to his feet, restless, pacing the chamber. His fingers trailed over the walls, carved with sigils older than the Academy itself. The stone was cool, etched with intricate whorls of dragon script and arcane patterns.

"I will find a way," he swore to himself. "I'll find something."

His fingertips brushed a line of designs, and he froze. The grooves beneath his touch thrummed, faintly alive. On instinct, words slipped from his lips—not in his own voice, not even in the language he knew. Ancient syllables rolled out, sharp and foreign.

The wall shivered.

With a low hum, the stone parted. A narrow compartment revealed itself, hidden deep within the chamber's frame.

Tariel's pulse thundered. He stepped closer, shadows bending as the small hollow glimmered faintly. Inside, something rested.

His breath caught. "Is that… what I think it is?"

And then another thought struck him, colder still.

That language again. The one no one else spoke. The one no one else even remembered. And yet the words came to him as naturally as breathing. He not only spoke them—he understood them.

How? How could he know a tongue that should have been lost to time?

Far above the Academy's dining hall, in a hidden chamber reinforced with ancient charms, the Dragon Council of the West had gathered.

Mariah Mac Naught sat at the head of the obsidian table, her silver hair gleaming in the sunlight. Her sharp eyes scanned the room, noting the tension carved into every line of her fellow council members' faces. She felt it too, a storm brewing, not of weather, but of prophecy.

She had been dreading this moment for years. Ever since the scrolls foretold the return of Tynan, a demon of darkness and chaos bound to the underworld, Mariah had watched for signs. She had been looking for any signs of unusual wear or cracks in the old seals or even a dragonborn child awakening with power that should not exist.

And now, it had happened.

"The Hell's Fire Dragon has awakened," she said, her voice calm but laced with finality. "Even if only partially, the signs are undeniable."

Septimus Reed, ever the harbinger of doom, leaned forward. "There is no partial awakening with a Hell's Fire dragon. That kind of power… it isn't born. It's summoned. Her existence means Tynan is on the move."

Mariah's jaw tightened. Tynan. One of the four infernal generals beneath Satan himself. While the other three remained dormant in the deeper circles of Hell, Tynan was always the most eager, the one who thirsted for blood and dominion.

In the dragon shapeshifters' circle, it was known through a prophecy that Tynan would arrive first. *The moment the Hell's Fire Dragon ascends, the veil will tear. Tynan shall step forth, and Satan's era will follow.*

In the age of the Celestial Reckoning, when the great war waged between the forces of Heaven and the demons of Hell for dominion over the three realms, the Hell's Fire Dragon had been a force of unmatched devastation. It was said the beast scorched battlefields with a single breath, its rage so fierce it wounded even the Heavenly God of War. Should the dragon rise again, war would be inevitable, the kind not seen since the Scorch Wars, when the last Hell's Fire Dragon turned cities to cinders and carved through legions like a living inferno.

She is the vessel. Mariah thought bitterly. *If he anchors himself to her, the world will bleed before Heaven can answer.*

But out loud, she said, "We must act. If the demon is preparing to rise, the vessel must be dealt with before it becomes a gateway."

Professor Fenwick's voice broke the stillness. "Several weeks ago, she didn't even know that she was of dragon lineage, a shapeshifter. She is still a child. Not a gateway. Not a weapon. She hasn't chosen Tynan. She doesn't even understand what she is."

Mariah met his gaze, finding no fear there, only pleading.

"She is the first of her kind in centuries," said Bevington Senior, his tone hard. "And her kind led to the great Scorch Wars between heavenly immortals and demons of Hell. Her very existence is dangerous."

"Punishing her for a form she never chose is not justice," Fenwick said, standing straighter now. "We've become the monsters we claim to fight."

"She has not hurt anyone," Professor Stark countered. "She needs guidance, not judgment."

Mariah was silent for a long moment. She understood Fenwick's point, truly, she did. But this was bigger than one girl. It was about the balance between realms. The veil between Earth and Hell was thinning, and if Tynan stepped through, he would not come alone.

Still, something in her hesitated. Perhaps there was one last chance to contain this.

Just then, the heavy door creaked open.

Tariel's heart pounded.

His fingers curled tightly around the ancient book, its weight digging into his arms, but he barely noticed. All he could feel was the burn in his chest, urgency, fear, and resolve.

He reached the doors of the meeting chamber in the Academy and didn't stop to second-guess himself.

"Wait!" he shouted, and his voice echoed like thunder across the high stone walls.

Every head turned. Robes shifted. Eyes widened. Gasps followed like ripples in water.

Tariel stepped forward, face flushed, spine rigid with determination. He was keenly aware of the gravity of what he was doing, interrupting the most powerful council in the realm, but he couldn't let them decide her fate. Not without this.

In his arms, the Book of Dracos seemed to hum, ancient and alive. He felt the thrum of its magic still tingling through his veins.

His father, Professor Fenwick, stood to the side, his voice low and stunned.

"Tariel?"

Tariel didn't waver.

"I found it," he said, his voice clearer than he expected. "The Book of Dracos has answers. It revealed itself to me in the Chamber of Meditation."

That part was true. The way the stone had shifted—the light. The book was there, as if it had been waiting for him.

Mariah Mac Naught, Chief of the Council, narrowed her sharp, silver eyes. "That book is a legend," she said, each word like a test.

Professor Stark stepped forward, her gaze scanning the book's worn cover. "It's real," she said. "The language is Draconian. Old and pure."

Mariah's gaze snapped back to Tariel. "And you can read it?"

Tariel swallowed, but he held his ground. "Yes. I taught my-self. I've studied every dialect I could find, spent nights dig-ging through forgotten records. This book is not just knowl-edge. It's a path. A guide for dragons like Everin."

He didn't say it, but he felt it: maybe even a guide for himself. Behind him, his father took a slow step forward, voice steady. "We ask for time. Let Everin learn who she is before you decide what she'll become."

Tariel's pulse roared in his ears. His legs felt heavy beneath the weight of so many eyes, of so much judgment. He could feel the skepticism in the room like a storm pressing in.

What if they didn't believe him? What if he was too late?

But then, finally, Mariah leaned back in her seat, her fingers tapping against the stone armrest in thought.

Long, tense silence stretched.

Mariah's silver eyes narrowed, sharp as blades. She didn't rise, but her voice carried enough weight to silence the entire chamber. "So what does this book say about the Hell's Fire Dragon?" she asked slowly, each word deliberate. "Is there any way to stop Tynan?"

Skepticism curled around her tone like frost.

Tariel's throat tightened.

He'd been waiting for that question.

CHAPTER 25

Plans to Control the Transformation

Tariel's fingers trembled slightly as he turned the time-worn pages of the Book of Dracos, the yellowed parchment whispering against his skin. His pulse thundered in his ears, louder than the murmurs of the council seated around him. The room still smelled of incense smoke and ancient magic, like something waiting to be disturbed.

He had to find something. Anything.

His eyes scanned symbols only he could read, desperate to retrieve the page he had skimmed before rushing into the chamber. And then, there it was.

He read aloud, voice hushed and taut with urgency.

"The Stone of Opalia... capable of subduing the beast inside the Hell's Fire Dragon. Said to temper violent transformations and to anchor the dragon soul to its human vessel. But the stone is lost, its trail buried beneath time in the depths of the ancient city once called Nyorica."

He paused, breath catching.

The remnants of old dragon history were rumored to be hidden in plain sight among human museums and ruins, preserved as clues, artifacts, and forgotten relics disguised as mythology.

A Council member asked, "Nyorica?"

"Before it became New York, it was known as Nyorica, the final stronghold during the Scorch Wars," Tariel murmured. "If the Stone of Opalia is hidden anywhere, it's buried beneath that city. There are fragmented directions," Tariel continued. "References to a particular museum known to carry ancient draconic artifacts, some with ties to the Scorch Wars. It is vague, but if we cross-reference with the archives..." He trailed off, already forming a plan.

Professor Stark stepped forward from the council circle. "Do you think you can locate it?"

Tariel looked up at her, then to the council members watching him with equal parts suspicion and intrigue.

"I do. We'll need to decode the rest of this entry, but I can read this language better than anyone else here right now," he said, more confidently than he felt. "It might take time, but if this stone is real, it could suppress Everin's transformation and stop Tynan's influence before it takes full hold."

"She doesn't need suppression," grumbled Elder Septimus, his tone like grinding stone. "She needs extermination. This is a fool's errand."

Headmaster Fenwick rose from his seat beside the council, his voice cool and steady. "No, Septimus. You know what she is, but you haven't seen who she is. I've met her. She's not a monster."

Another council member's expression darkened. "And if she loses control?"

"She won't," Tariel cut in. All eyes turned to him again. "Not if we help her. That stone is the key. If there's a chance, even a small one, I'm taking it."

A murmur spread through the council.

Mariah Mac Naught hadn't spoken yet. She sat still at the head of the chamber, hands folded, her eyes unreadable, her long braid of silver hair gleaming in the lanternlight. The councilors around her shifted, their robes brushing against stone as murmurs flickered through the chamber.

Finally, she let her voice cut through the air. "And you're sure this isn't another myth?"

Her tone was low, skeptical, and dangerous.

Across the circle, Tariel held her gaze with more defiance than caution. "Myths carry truth, at least enough to start with. And I'm not asking for blind trust, only a little time for one mission. Let me try."

Silence answered him.

Then Bevington Senior leaned forward, fingers steepled. "He's bold. Like his mother."

Mariah noticed the flicker in Tariel's eyes. The words had caught him off guard, though he covered it quickly.

Mariah let the moment stretch before she exhaled, slow and deliberate. "Fine. One week. Take your team and retrieve this Stone of Opalia, if it exists. But be warned, Tariel Fenwick, if you return empty-handed, the Council will act."

He nodded once. "Understood."

The council shifted again, murmurs resuming, some doubtful, some intrigued. But Mariah stayed still, her face a mask.

Inside, her thoughts sharpened like a blade. She didn't believe for a moment that chasing after a lost stone in some human city would change anything. The Hell's Fire Dragon was not a problem to be soothed or suppressed. It was a curse to be eradicated, the only way to ensure Tynan never returned.

But if she said so now, Fenwick and Stark would rise in protest, arguing for compassion, mercy, and hope. Better to give the boy his week. Let him chase myths, let him fail. When he returned empty-handed, as she knew he would, the Council would see what she saw. That no charm, no relic, no stone could save the Hell's Fire Dragon.

Then her hand would be stronger and her voice undeniable.

Outside the chamber, as the heavy doors groaned shut behind him, Tariel finally allowed himself a shaky breath.

One week.

The words rang in his head like a tolling bell. One week to prove them wrong. One week to keep Everin safe. One week before the Council decided her fate without mercy.

He gripped the Book of Dracos tighter to his chest, feeling the thrum of power still pulsing in its spine. For Everin. For the Academy. For all of them.

The latch clicked again, and Headmaster Fenwick stepped out, his face grave but steady. He laid a hand briefly on Tariel's shoulder. "Tell Everin she's needed in my office," he said quietly. "Now." His eyes softened. "And I'm proud of you, Tariel."

Tariel nodded, pulling out his phone as his dad disappeared down the corridor. His fingers hovered for a moment before he typed.

You're wanted in Fenwick's office. Don't worry, I'll be with you. Whatever happens, we'll work it out together. I'm with you.

He hit send, staring at the screen until the message whooshed away.

Then he tightened his hold on the Book of Dracos, squared his shoulders, and walked on.

Everin stood before the tall, arched door of the Headmaster's office, her hands damp with nervous sweat. Her heart was still unsettled after everything that had happened during the day: the whispers, the fear in everyone's eyes, the power inside her that felt like a storm barely contained. And now, this.

She took a breath and pushed the door open.

The office was filled with quiet tension.

The late afternoon sun streamed through the wide stained-glass windows, casting dragon-shaped patterns across the floor. Shelves of ancient tomes and rare relics lined the walls, and in the center of the room stood Headmaster Fenwick be-hind his heavy desk, his expression calm and unreadable.

Tariel turned the moment she entered, his eyes locking with hers. A small smile tugged at the corner of his lips, and some-thing inside Everin softened. Tariya stood beside him, arms crossed but alert, while Professor Stark flipped through a file, her expression sharp with focus, and Professor Rudiff watched quietly with his arms clasped behind his back.

"Come in, Everin," Headmaster Fenwick said, signaling her

closer to where Tariel and Tariya stood. "We were waiting for you."

Everin stood beside them, trying not to let her racing thoughts show. She could feel Tariel's steady presence at her side, and that helped more than she wanted to admit.

The Headmaster's voice turned serious. "The Council has approved a mission to retrieve the Stone of Opalia. We believe it's the only artifact powerful enough to help you contain your transformation before it becomes something far more dangerous."

Everin nodded slightly, her stomach twisting. She didn't need anyone to tell her how dangerous she might become. She felt it burning inside her.

"But not everyone can go," Fenwick continued. "Phoenix Bevington has been forbidden to join by her father. He made that decision personally and firmly. She will remain here under supervision."

Everin blinked in surprise. She hadn't expected that. Phoenix had always been ready for an adventure.

"Jackson Miller is still new to the dragon community," Professor Rudiff added, glancing at Everin. "We're not sure he's ready to face what might lie beneath Nyorica."

Everin saw Tariel's jaw clench slightly at that.

"But he's strong," she said before she could stop herself. "He's more capable than most."

The Headmaster didn't argue, but his tone didn't waver. "The Council has made its recommendations. This mission requires precision, subtlety, and focus."

Tariya stepped forward. "Then who is going?"

Fenwick's gaze swept across the room. "You, Tariya. And Tariel. And Everin."

Professor Stark inclined her head toward Tariya. "You are the best shapeshifter in your grade, fast, precise, and adaptable."

Professor Rudiff's eyes moved to Tariel. "Mrs. Inkpen believes you are the best at reading Draconian texts fluently. That skill alone could mean the difference between success and failure."

The Headmaster's gaze settled on Everin. "And you must go because we do not know how long before you fully transform. The sooner you obtain the Stone of Opalia, the better chance you have of controlling your dragon form."

Professor Stark added, "I will oversee the smooth running of things during your quest. You all answer to me."

Rudiff gave a short nod. "I'm proficient in combat, and I'll ensure we all make it back in one piece."

A strange cocktail of fear and purpose settled in Everin's chest. She hadn't expected to be given a chance to contain her dragon.

"We've arranged for transport," the Headmaster went on. "Tomorrow morning, you'll drive to the town of Vallenshire, about an hour from here. A small private aircraft will be waiting to fly you into New York City. From there, you'll be guided discreetly to the museum that houses the ruins of ancient Nyorica, where the Stone may be hidden beneath."

Everin exchanged a glance with Tariel. There was so much to take in, but the thing that stuck in her mind was the trust they were placing in him. In them. In her.

She swallowed. "And what happens if we don't find it?"

Professor Stark said calmly, "Then we keep searching. But you must go in believing you will, because the alternative is not in your favor."

The Headmaster looked at Tariel for a long moment, then added slowly, "Tariel, you'll be far from home, and I'm trusting you with everything."

His words lingered in the air.

Everin felt the weight of them.

She wasn't sure what lay beneath the streets of New York or if they'd truly find the Stone of Opalia. But as she looked at the team around her, and the fire burning quietly behind Tariel's eyes, she felt something unexpected.

Hope.

That night, Everin sat cross-legged on her bed, a half-packed satchel lying open beside her. Across the room, Tariya was neatly folding clothes into her own bag, humming under her breath, while Phoenix sat on her bed with her arms crossed, muttering about "stupid family rules" and "missing all the fun."

Everin was about to ask if Tariya had seen her travel cloak when her phone buzzed against the blanket.

Her heart skipped a beat when she saw the name flashing on the screen.

Dad.

He rarely called.

She swiped to answer. "Hi, Dad."

There was a pause on the other end, then his familiar, deep voice. "I've been informed by the Academy. You're going to New York."

Everin tightened her grip on the phone. "Yeah... I am."

Another pause. Then, quietly, "Are you afraid?"

She exhaled slowly. "A little." She almost said a lot, but she didn't want him to worry.

"You should be," he said, not unkindly. "Fear keeps you sharp. But don't let it own you." His tone grew firmer. "If your dragon is a problem for the world, then you fight it, even if that means you fight yourself."

Everin stared at the floor, her throat tightening. "What if I can't win?"

"Then you keep trying until you do."

The simple certainty in his voice steadied something inside her.

He went on, softer now. "Listen to me, Everin. Whether you come back with that Stone or not, I'm with you. Always. You're my daughter before you're any dragon."

Her eyes stung, and she pressed her lips together, willing herself not to cry. "Thanks, Dad."

"Go get some sleep," he said. "You've got a big day tomorrow."

When the call ended, Everin sat there for a long moment, phone still in her hand, the sound of his voice echoing in her mind.

Her screen lit up again. This time it was a message from Tariel.

Tariel: Still packing?
Everin: Yeah. You?
Tariel: Almost done. Just wanted to say... tomorrow's going to be a lot. But you won't be alone. I've got you. Always.

Everin: ...Thanks. That means more than you know.

Tariel: Get some rest, Hell's Fire girl. You'll need it.

Everin: You too, dragon boy.

A faint smile tugged at her lips as she set her phone aside.

Across the room, Phoenix's voice cracked as she spoke. "I'm going to miss you both," she said, blinking rapidly. "I wish I didn't come from the Bevington family. They always think they know best."

Tariya gave her a sympathetic smile. "We'll be back before you know it."

Before either of them could respond, Phoenix suddenly pulled both girls into a fierce hug. "Just... don't do anything stupid without me, okay?"

Everin laughed softly, hugging her back. "No promises."

Phoenix's sniffle turned into a shaky laugh. "I'm serious."

And for the first time in days, Everin felt stronger.

CHAPTER 26

Shadows in the City

The wealthy, pristine end of New York felt like another world to Everin.

Glass towers sliced into the pale winter sky, their mirrored windows catching shards of sunlight. Crowds bustled past in tailored coats, their polished shoes clicking across clean pavement. Everything gleamed here—shop windows, spotless sidewalks, even the air seemed to hum with money and order.

It made her feel small and out of place. She had grown up in Midows, New York, but she had never walked this far into the city's wealthy heart. Here, nothing felt familiar, except Tariel's steady figure walking ahead with the others close behind.

The Museum of Ancient Artifacts rose before them like a monument to another age. Its stone façade was carved with dragons in flight, and its bronze doors were dark with age.

Inside, the air was cooler and sharper, and the sound of their footsteps seemed too loud. Everin frowned. For a Saturday afternoon, the place felt wrong. Too quiet.

A few uniformed employees lingered near the far walls, watching them with polite, fixed smiles that didn't reach their eyes. Something about them made her skin prickle.

The team spread out, scanning every display for a clue to the Stone of Opalia. Glass cases held relics that glimmered under pale lights. These were old blades, scrolls sealed beneath protective charms, and small dragon sculptures worn smooth by age. Tariya moved quickly from plaque to plaque, her eyes darting for keywords, while Professor Stark prowled between exhibits, muttering about how most of the collection was padded with fakes rather than true draconic artifacts.

Everin paused at a carved obsidian dragon with green-fire eyes. It seemed to stare back at her, almost as if daring her to keep searching.

"This was a waste of time," Professor Stark said under her breath, snapping a case shut.

Everin's reply never came, because a sound, soft but deliberate, caught her ear. A faint rustle from the back hall.

She turned, heart skipping.

From the dim corridor beyond the exhibits, six figures emerged as men and women in black suits moved in perfect formation. Their leader strode ahead, tall and broad-shouldered, with slick black hair and a smile that didn't belong anywhere near warmth. Energy shimmered around his hands like heat above a fire pit.

"Boss Kael," one of the suited figures murmured.

Kael's gaze fixed on her. "There she is."

A fireball bloomed in his palm and shot across the space.

Everin dove aside, the heat searing her cheek as it smashed into a marble pillar. The museum erupted. Employees shouted, some bolting for the doors, others ducking behind displays. As Everin sprinted past a fleeing staff member, the woman looked up, her pupils narrowing into vertical slits before she vanished into the crowd.

Dragons. They were dragons too.

The thought barely had time to settle when without warning, weapons appeared as sleek, black-barreled guns spat long streaks of red light.

"Cover!" Professor Stark shouted, springing sideways.

Professor Rudiff met the rush head-on, his palms igniting as he batted away blasts and kicked one attacker into a glass case. Shards exploded across the floor.

"Everin, come with me!" Tariya yanked her behind a stone display just as another shot scorched the marble where she had been standing.

Tariel slid in beside them. "We have to move. Now!"

They ducked between exhibits, as Tariya threw a sweep kick at one of the men who lunged at her. Everin spun at her call—"Left!"—kicking another in the gut hard enough to drop him. Kael's voice rang out behind them. "Don't let her out of the building!"

But they were already running.

The glass doors burst open, releasing a rush of sound as honking cars, chattering tourists, and the steady stream of city life greeted them. They pushed into the crowd, weaving between startled pedestrians.

For a moment, Everin thought they would lose them in the noise. But when she glanced back, Kael and two of his men were still there, slipping through the bodies as if they had been trained for it.

Tariel caught her wrist. "This way!"

Tariya followed.

They cut down a side street, the noise of the main avenue faded, and shadows pooled between old brick buildings. The street narrowed into an alleyway, and that was when a tall figure stepped from the darkness.

"Get down!"

Everin dropped instantly and so did Tariel and Tariya.

A wall of fire roared past her, forcing Kael and his men to stumble back, shielding their faces. The alley lit in violent orange, shadows jerking against the walls.

She looked up, heart hammering. "Dad?"

"Stay close," ordered Marcus.

With his fire clearing the path, they slipped through a back way, twisting down darkened streets until the city noise swallowed their pursuers.

Only when they stepped inside an abandoned apartment building did Everin finally breathe again.

Everin asked, "Dad, how did you find me?"

Marcus Haydon's eyes softened just a little. "Family GPS tracking app, which all our family members have installed on their cell phones. I just had this feeling you were in danger. After I heard about the Hell's Fire Dragon, I couldn't stay away. When the Academy told me you would be in New York, I took leave and followed. I needed to see you with my own eyes."

"I'll contact the professors," said Tariel, taking his cell phone out.

"With this gang tracking us, our accommodation booked for the night will not be safe. But I have a place in mind," informed Tariya.

Everin realised the danger had passed, for now, but for how long before the gang caught with them, she wasn't sure.

That night, the team camped out in an apartment owned by Tariya's family. The Grattons were out of town, and Tariya had insisted they use it as a safe place to rest and plan their next move. The rooms were sparsely furnished but warm enough to feel safe.

They sat around a small table, sharing a simple dinner. Professor Rudiff cleared his throat. "We need to think about our next move," he said. "I know we've been looking for the Stone of Opalia here in New York, but there's a place that holds more knowledge than anything we've seen so far, the Archives of the Dragon Council."

The room fell silent. Everyone knew the Archives were the most secure part of the Council's headquarters. They held the oldest, most powerful texts on dragon lore.

"If we can get access," Rudiff continued, "we might find more on the Stone. Something that could tell us exactly where it is."

"Why didn't they let us search the Archives in the first place? I mean… if I'm a brewing danger to the whole world…" Everin's voice trailed off. She didn't want to say the rest.

"Because some members of the Council believe the Hell's Fire Dragon should be wiped out," Professor Stark said. Her voice was steady. "To prevent its master, the Demon of Darkness and Chaos, from rising at all."

"So they just want to kidnap my daughter," Marcus muttered, his tone sharp.

Tariel's gaze shifted to Everin then, almost instinctively. For a moment, the sounds in the room seemed to fade away. His eyes, which lingered on hers, were steady, warm, and certain, as if he was silently telling her that no matter what the Council decided, he wasn't going to let them touch her. She felt heat rise to her cheeks and quickly glanced down at her hands, but the comfort in that look stayed with her, easing the tightness in her chest.

"We'll need to get there as soon as possible," Tariel said, his tone firm but carrying the same quiet assurance she had just seen in his eyes. "We don't have much time. We're already being hunted."

"And we need a plan," said Tariya, bringing in her laptop.

Everin nodded. The danger was real, and every step they took could be their last. But she wasn't going to back down, not when Tariel's unspoken promise was still warm in her mind, and not when so much depended on finding the Stone of Opalia. She only hoped it wasn't already too late.

CHAPTER 27

A Secret Vault

The next morning, the group gathered in the modest apartment to prepare for their next step. Marcus Haydon was getting ready to leave. Everin stood by the window, staring out at the early morning light breaking over the skyline, her thoughts tangled in worry. She had never seen her father in such a hurry before, and the sudden parting left her feeling unsettled.

Marcus placed a hand on her shoulder, his grip warm and firm.

"Everin," he said, his voice low but steady. "Be careful. You don't know who you can trust here, because not everyone has your best interest at heart." His eyes, filled with both love and concern, held hers. "If anything happens, call me. I'll be there."

Everin nodded, swallowing the lump in her throat. "I'll be careful, Dad. Thank you."

"Good," he said, pulling her into a tight hug. "And stay strong. Don't let anyone tell you who you are, especially when you don't even know yourself yet."

With that, he was gone, leaving the apartment quieter and heavier.

Tariel was in the kitchen, his back turned as he busied himself with a frying pan. The smell of sizzling bacon drifted through the air, making Everin's stomach grumble. She couldn't help but admire him as he worked, the easy confidence in his movements, the way the morning light seemed to catch in his dark hair. He looked effortlessly handsome, and her heart gave a soft ache as her feelings for him only deepened.

"Need some help?" she asked, stepping into the warm light of the kitchen.

Tariel glanced over his shoulder, a small smile tugging at his lips. "If you want to help, keep me company. I could use the moral support. And maybe be a taste tester if you're feeling brave."

She arched an eyebrow. "Brave, huh? That doesn't sound very reassuring."

He chuckled, whisking eggs with practiced ease. "My cooking

will be better than last time, I promise."

"That wouldn't be hard to beat," she teased, brushing past him to set two plates on the counter. "Last night, I couldn't tell if it was chicken or rubber."

Tariel laughed, the sound warm. "Okay, fair. But in my defense, I was busy trying not to burn the Grattons' apartment."

The easy banter eased something tight inside her. For a few minutes, the weight of the world seemed to lift, and it was just them, two partners in a quiet kitchen pretending life was normal.

Tariel slid the eggs onto the plates and set the pan aside. When she turned to take them, her fingers brushed his. She looked up and found his gaze waiting for hers. It was steady, searching, carrying a silent promise that he would be there, no matter what came next.

Before she could think, he leaned in, and she met him halfway. The kiss was soft, not rushed or demanding, just an unspoken reassurance, a way of telling each other that somehow, everything would be alright.

When they pulled apart, her heart was racing, but not from fear.

"Come on," he said quietly, handing her a plate. "Eat. We have a long day ahead."

She nodded, unable to hide the small, private smile tugging at her lips.

By the time breakfast was done, the mood had shifted back to urgency. The team was ready to leave, and the journey to the Council of Dragons of the West was about to begin.

The Drakon Academy team hopped off the tram and walked a short distance to the Mascott Building, a common name in the human world, but only the dragon community knew what lay within the walls. The building housing the Council of Dragons of the West loomed in front of them, its grandeur impossible to ignore. Tall marble columns lined the entrance, and the golden dragon insignia inscribed above the doors was a clear reminder of the power held within.

Everin took a deep breath, trying to quell the growing sense of intimidation. She had no idea what to expect inside, only that it was going to be difficult to get answers.

Professor Stark stood at the head of the group, her posture rigid and formal as she approached the entrance. "Stick to the plan," she instructed, her voice low but commanding. "We're here to submit the Book of Dracos, as instructed by Lady Mac Naught. Nothing more, nothing less. We don't want to draw any unnecessary attention."

Mr. Zenith, the manager of the Council's building, a pompous man in his forties, greeted them in the lobby with an air of skepticism. His bald head gleamed under the overhead lights as he adjusted his glasses and eyed them warily.

"Do you have the Book of Dracos?" he asked, his tone businesslike.

Professor Stark smiled coolly, lifting the book in her hands. "Yes, of course," she said, her voice smooth as silk. "We've been instructed by Lady Mac Naught herself to bring it for review."

Zenith looked at the book, his expression unreadable. "Hmm. It's been a while since the Council has requested such a thing." He eyed them suspiciously. "I'll need to see it before you can go any further."

Miss Stark didn't hesitate, her hand moving quickly to open the book, revealing its ancient pages. Zenith's eyes widened slightly at the sight of the text, the strange symbols and mysterious writings clearly drawing his interest. After a moment of tense silence, he nodded reluctantly.

"Very well," he muttered. "Follow me."

The group followed Mr. Zenith through the long, echoing corridors of the Council of Dragons of the West building, their footsteps soft against the polished marble floors. Tariel's eyes never stopped moving, taking in the carved doorframes, the gilded dragon motifs glinting in the lamplight, the subtle turns of the hallways. This place was a palace of history and politics, and every wall seemed to hum with the weight of centuries.

They turned another corner, and his gaze caught on the words carved in gold above an arched doorway: **The Archives**. The lettering was bold yet elegant, as if deliberately meant to draw the eye. He didn't need to say a word. One look at Everin, then at Tariya, was enough. They all understood. This was where they needed to be. Not now, not with Zenith watching, but soon.

Inside Zenith's office, the atmosphere was heavy, as though the very air was aware of the politics at play. Professor Stark and Professor Rudiff were seated opposite Zenith, speaking in low, deliberate tones about the Book of Dracos. The ancient tome rested on the polished surface between them, looking as though it belonged in this place of power.

Zenith leaned back in his chair with the posture of a man who was used to respect. Tariel stepped forward with an easy expression, pretending to examine the Book's pages before reading a few lines aloud in the pure Dracos tongue. The effect was immediate. Zenith's brows rose, and his earlier indifference shifted into genuine curiosity.

"You can read ancient Dracos?" Zenith asked, leaning forward, his tone betraying a trace of admiration.

"A hobby," Tariel replied mildly, the corners of his mouth twitching upward.

As Zenith leaned in, Tariel's right hand moved in a fluid, practiced motion. The passkey slid out of Zenith's pocket with barely a whisper. His heart thudded once in satisfaction, but his face remained composed.

Across the room, Everin suddenly stumbled back, her breath sharp. She clutched at herself as if wrestling with something inside.

"Oh no! I... I can't control it!" she cried, her voice rising in alarm.

Zenith's chair scraped hard against the floor as he shot to his feet. "What's wrong with her?"

From behind, Tariel heard Professor Stark's dry voice. "She's learning her transformation and is unable to control it yet. You don't want her burning your office."

Tariya was already at Everin's side, her grip firm on her friend's arm. "Come on, let's get you some air," she said quickly, playing her part without missing a beat.

"Stay calm," Tariel added, stepping in smoothly, urgency hidden beneath his steady tone.

The moment they turned into a side corridor, Tariya slipped her free hand into her jacket pocket and pulled out a small, sleek device no bigger than a coin. Tariel recognized it instantly: one of her uncle's toys, a gadget that could scramble or erase them from any live security feed. Highly illegal, highly effective. She pressed a stud on its side, and a faint ripple shimmered over them like heat haze. Tariel knew they could move now without leaving a trace.

The corridor to the Archives was deserted. He slid the passkey into the lock, and the door opened with a quiet click.

The air inside was thick and cool, smelling faintly of parchment and old leather bindings. Shelves lined the walls, heavy with scrolls and ancient books, the kind of relics whose value couldn't be measured in gold. But nothing they could see hinted at the Stone.

It was Everin who noticed the massive dragon banner hanging against the far wall, its edges shifting slightly in a draft. She pulled it aside to reveal a stone door carved with faded runes.

The door swung inward, and they stepped into a smaller vault. Here, the air seemed older still, heavy with the kind of silence that only came from being sealed away for decades. Glass display cases lined the walls, filled with relics whose markings even Tariel couldn't place. But at the very back, incongruous among all the ancient wonders, sat a sleek computer terminal.

Before Tariel could process what he was seeing, Tariya was at the desk, her fingers flying across the keyboard. He had no idea where she'd learned to move like that, but she was damn good. She slid a slim USB stick from her pocket and plugged it into the side of the machine. The screen flickered, lines of encrypted code unraveling under her touch as if the system itself were bowing to her will.

Minutes later, the database opened like a vault door, revealing rows of records and catalogues. Tariya's eyes scanned the entries until she stopped suddenly.

"The Stone of Opalia," she read aloud, her voice tight. "Last seen in St. Paul's Chapel, located within Columbus College."

A flicker of triumph shot through Tariel's chest. They had their lead.

"We need to move," he said sharply. "Zenith won't be distracted forever."

They left the vault as they had entered, quiet, careful, and without a trace, with Tariel locking the door behind them. Walking swiftly, he let the passkey fall to the floor in the shadows, his mind already turning to their next step.

St. Paul's Chapel. Columbus College.

Now they finally had a direction.

Later that night, the three of them sat together on the sofa in Gratton's apartment, the hum of the city outside faint through the windows. Professor Stark and Professor Rudiff faced each other from opposite chairs, their voices low but charged.

"It's too risky," Professor Stark said, her tone clipped.

Mr. Rudiff leaned forward, elbows on his knees. "It's our only lead. If we want the Stone of Opalia, we have to move now. The Council will waste days debating while our enemies close in."

Tariya crossed her arms. "He's right. We can't just sit here."

Tariel gave a small nod. "Waiting only gives them an advantage."

Everin kept her gaze on Rudiff, grateful someone was willing to push for action. "We can handle it," she said quietly.

Professor Stark's eyes moved over each of them before she let out a long sigh. "Fine. We leave for Columbus College tomorrow. But we stay sharp. One mistake could ruin everything."

Everin felt the words settle heavily inside her. Tomorrow could change everything, for better or worse.

CHAPTER 28

How Not to Be?

The tingling started before dawn. Everin woke with her skin prickling, her heartbeat loud in her ears. Each thump sent heat through her veins. She lay still, willing it to fade. But it didn't.

A sharp pulse shot up her spine. She gasped and sat up. Her fingers curled on their own. Points of pain broke the skin, and claws replaced her nails. The room tilted, edges bending like heat waves.

"Everin?" Tariya's voice came from the next bed, sleep-blurred but worried.

"Are you okay?"

Everin slid her feet to the floor and tried to breathe. "Stay back," she said.

Tariya crossed the rug anyway and reached for her shoulder. Everin's arm swept out, not to strike but to keep her away. Power surged, and Tariya flew backward, hitting the wall with a thud. She slid down, stunned, then held up a hand to show she was fine. She didn't come closer.

The pressure inside Everin climbed. Dark heat coiled through her bones. She caught her reflection in the dresser mirror and froze. Green fire burned in her eyes, scales pushed through her skin, and each scale carried the hell's mark, a dark, forked flame glyph.

Footsteps pounded down the hall.

The door flew open. Professor Stark, Professor Rudiff, and Tariel rushed in. Stark took it all in at a glance: Tariya on the floor, and Everin half-shifted. Her mouth set as she figured out what had happened moments ago.

Rudiff stepped forward, golden light already building in his hands. Threads of dragon energy spun outward, weaving into a net that dropped over Everin and tightened. The restraint clamped down hard. She snarled, a sound that didn't feel human.

"Hold," Stark said, voice clipped.

"I'm holding," Rudiff ground out.

The power inside her heaved. The net groaned and split. Golden strands snapped like brittle wire and fell away.

Everin's gaze locked on Rudiff, fierce and unblinking.

Tariel stepped in front of her. His lips moved. The words that came weren't modern Draconian. They were deeper, older tones that seemed to hang in the air. The sound reached her, not like a command but like a hand offered through smoke.

She understood what he meant: Stay with me. Don't go under.

"I won't be controlled," she hissed in the same ancient Draconian language, her voice layered, half hers and half something else.

Tariel's eyes moved a fraction as he comprehended what she had said, but before he could speak further, the Professors acted.

Rudiff surged his magic again. A second net crashed down, thicker and brighter. Stark added her power, anchoring it. The pressure closed in from all sides until the heat receded. Claws withdrew. Scales sank. Everin dropped to her knees, chest heaving.

Silence held for a beat. Stark's eyes cut to Tariel. "What language was that?"

Rudiff shook his head. "Older than anything I've heard in practice."

Tariya asked curiously, "And what did you say to each other?"

Everin swallowed. "I've heard him speak it before. It feels… tied to the ancient dragons. The powerful ones." She didn't say anything about the underground alpha dragon, Braskora.

Tariel's brow furrowed. "I don't even know what I said."

Everin let Tariel's lie slide for now, though she noticed Tariya wasn't convinced either.

The fear didn't ease. The pressure hadn't vanished; it pressed the edges of her ribs. Everin's voice came out small and hoarse. "I don't know how to stop it. I feel it inside me—the Hell's Fire Dragon. And there's something else, darker and stronger. I'm nothing beside it. It keeps pushing, like it's ordering me to wake up and let everything loose."

Tariel's jaw tightened. "Is it Tynan, the demon of darkness and chaos?"

Tariya, still braced against the wall, spoke dryly. "What else could command a Hell's Fire Dragon? She's one of hell's strongest."

Stark and Rudiff traded a look that said the same thing neither wanted to voice. Rudiff eased the net just enough for Everin to sit back against the bed frame.

"Once you fully transform," he said quietly, certainty hardening his tone, "Tynan will awaken. He's linked to you now. When you shift completely, there's no turning back."

Tariel didn't move away from her. "So we're in a race against time?"

Stark nodded. "Yes. Two days at most. Maybe less. If we don't find a way to stop this, Everin loses control and Tynan walks free. After that…" She let the rest hang.

Everin stared at her hands. They still shook. "I don't want to hurt anyone," she whispered. "It feels like I'm slipping. What if I can't stop it? What if I become his puppet?"

Tariel stepped closer and lowered his voice. "You're not him. You're you. We'll find a way. I swear."

The net hummed softly as Rudiff held it. The room smelled

faintly of singed air and lemon cleaner. Tariya pushed herself up and gave Everin a small, steady nod from across the room.

The thing inside Everin prowled and waited.

Time, she knew, had just become their most dangerous ene-my.

The streets of New York bustled with noise and movement, but none of it reached the tight coil of focus inside Everin. Columbus College stood ahead, its ivy-covered stone walls and arched windows lending it an air of age and prestige. Students hurried across the courtyard, books under their arms, as laughter spilled into the crisp air. For a brief moment, the scene almost felt normal. Almost.

They kept moving. Professor Rudiff and Professor Stark went toward the principal's office to deal with visitor formalities. It was just a cover. The real goal waited for Everin, Tariel, and Tariya: St. Paul's Church, hidden deep within the college grounds.

Students lounged on the lawns, tossing a Frisbee, sipping coffee, and talking in clusters. The everyday life unfolding around her felt so far from the world she knew. Tariel glanced at her, and the look he gave was steady, grounding. Tariya's sharp gaze swept their surroundings, alert for any threat.

The church's entrance was quiet, its arched doorway shadowed. Everin was just about to step inside when a sharp hiss cut through the air.

A young Asian woman leapt from the shadows, no older than her twenties, her movements fast and deliberate. Thin, gleaming needles shot from her hands in a deadly scatter. Her expression was calm, but her eyes were hard and calculating.

Tariya moved instantly, dragon magic rippling over her skin until it sheathed her in smooth, reflective scales. The needles struck and bounced harmlessly away, clinking against the stone steps.

Tariel was already in motion, meeting the attacker head-on. His movements were precise, each strike and dodge a mirror to hers. Everin's chest tightened as she joined in, the heat inside her surging upward, demanding release.

The woman flipped back into range, weapons ready. Everin let the force inside her burst outward. It was not fire but a wave that struck her opponent mid-spin and sent her stumbling.

"Stay back!" Tariel's voice was calm, but there was no mistaking the urgency.

The woman ignored him, lunging again. Tariel's kick met her mid-charge, sending her into the church wall with a heavy thud. She slid down, dazed but not out.

"Let's go!" Everin said, pushing against the church doors.

Tariya hesitated only a moment, watching the woman stir. "We'll be followed if we wait."

They slipped inside, the doors closing behind them. The dim, cool air wrapped around Everin, her pulse still thundering in her ears.

They were in.

For now.

CHAPTER 29

Into the Demon's Shadow

The heavy wooden doors of St. Paul's Church groaned shut behind them, and the quiet that settled over Tariel felt unnatural—too still, too aware. The air was thick with incense and the cold breath of stone that had stood there for centuries. He could hear their footsteps echo off the arched ceilings, each one swallowed by shadows that pooled in the corners.

Beautiful from the outside, yes, but beauty didn't mask what he felt humming under his skin. This place was old. Older than the college. Older than the city. And something inside it was awake.

The light from the stained glass spilled across the worn wooden benches, painting the aisle in muted colors. His eyes skimmed over the high arches and faded tapestries without lingering; they weren't here to admire anything. They were here for the Stone. Nothing else mattered.

"Where do we even start?" Everin whispered.

"We find the stone," he said, keeping his voice calm but clipped. "It's here somewhere."

They moved toward the altar. Tariel's gaze slid over an angel statue with eyes cast downward in prayer, but the stillness in its face didn't feel serene. It felt like scrutiny.

It was Tariya who broke the moment. "Look at this," she murmured.

In the far corner, shrouded in shadow, stood a figure far larger than the rest. Dark stone. Arms outstretched as if commanding obedience. Horns curled upward like the crown of some ancient beast. Tariel's stomach tightened.

"That's him," he said before Everin had even formulated her question. "Tynan."

Why here? Why in a church?

Tariya crouched, tracing the faint outline of a crack at the statue's base. "Help me push."

The stone resisted at first, then shifted with a grinding groan. Dust rained down. Beneath it, black stairs fell away into darkness. Stale, unmoving air rushed up to meet them, heavy with the scent of age. Cobwebs clung in thick ropes across the opening, shivering in the sudden disturbance.

Tariel exchanged a brief look with Everin. No words passed between them, only the silent agreement that they were going down. He drew his sapphire shaft, twisting the hilt until a pale blue light spilled from its tip. Everin followed suit, the glow from hers mingling with his, casting cold light down the stairwell.

They descended.

The stone steps were slick with moisture, their edges worn smooth by time. The sound of their footsteps felt muffled, as though the walls themselves were swallowing it whole. The passage wound downward until it opened into a tunnel where the floor lay under a sheet of still water, faintly luminescent.

A ripple broke the surface. Tariel felt it before he saw it: movement in the depths. Scales broke the water, green as tarnished bronze, eyes burning gold.

"Water serpent," Tariel hissed, tightening his grip on the sapphire shaft. Its faint blue glow caught the glint of scales sliding just beneath the surface, weaving like liquid shadows.

The creature broke the water with an explosion of spray, its head huge, and fangs curved like hooked daggers. The stench of rot rolled off it as it lunged, a blur of muscle and hunger.

It went for Tariya first. She reacted on instinct, her body snapping into her dragon form mid-stride, silver scales locking into place with a sound like cracking ice. The serpent's fangs clanged against her armor-like hide, the impact rattling through the water. She drove her shoulder into its jaw, slamming the beast sideways.

The tunnel erupted into chaos. Water crashed against the walls, drenching them. The serpent twisted with unnerving speed, coiling around Tariya's legs, trying to drag her under.

"Move!" Tariel barked, surging forward. He slammed the end of his shaft into the coils, forcing them to loosen, then swung upward in a sharp arc that cracked against the creature's head. It let out a wet, guttural hiss and whipped away, only to come snapping back toward him.

Tariel ducked, water churning past his face, and brought the shaft up under its jaw, redirecting it straight toward Everin.

Her eyes widened. She didn't think. She thrust both palms forward, summoning a sudden blast of heat. The water around her sizzled, steam billowing upward in a blinding cloud. The serpent reared back in shock, its movement slowed by the boiling surge.

"Now!" Tariel shouted.

Tariya ripped free of the coils, her claws flashing. She brought both hands down in a crushing blow to the serpent's skull. The impact sent vibrations shuddering through the water and into the stone walls.

The serpent thrashed wildly, its tail striking Tariel across the ribs and sending him staggering into the wall. Pain shot through his side, but he pushed off, driving his shaft into the creature's midsection, forcing it to turn again, straight into Tariya's waiting claws.

One final, savage strike split the guardian's head, and it convulsed before slipping under the surface. The water stilled, though the ripples carried the last of its fury into the shadows below.

Chest heaving, Tariel lowered his weapon, scanning the dark water. He didn't trust that it was truly gone.

Tariya shifted back, pale and dripping, her breathing ragged. "That was not just a serpent," she muttered. "It was guarding something."

Tariel exchanged a glance with Everin. She was still catching her breath, steam curling faintly from her hands. Whatever lay ahead, the temple wasn't going to give it up without a fight.

The water shallowed ahead, revealing a narrow walkway that led them to a massive underground chamber. The moment they stepped inside, the place lit itself. Candles and sconces flared to life along the walls, their flames burning steady despite the damp air.

Tariel's pulse tightened. *Does he know?*

The thought was unbidden, sharp. If Tynan's temple was reacting, then somewhere, somehow, the Demon of Darkness and Chaos was aware that the Hell's Fire Dragon had entered his domain. His gaze flicked to Everin, the flickering light catching in her hair. It wasn't as if they'd had a choice; she wouldn't have stayed behind even if they had tried to make her. Still, part of him wondered if they had just stepped into something they couldn't walk back from.

In the center of the chamber loomed a colossal statue of Tynan again, carved in dark stone, his face twisted into a smile that didn't belong to anything human. Horns spiraled high above a crown of tangled hair. His arms, outstretched, held a sword that seemed to gleam faintly in the candlelight.

"Is this his temple?" Tariel asked, though he already knew the answer.

"I think it is," Everin murmured.

"This isn't an accident," Tariel said, voice low. "Someone wanted us to find this place."

Everin moved forward. His gut tightened as her hand reached out, but before he could warn her, she touched the stone.

The scream ripped through the chamber, the sound bouncing off every wall. Tariel caught her before she fell, the heat in her skin like fire under his fingers. The statue's eyes glowed red. The stone cracked. And the air, thick with the weight of something ancient, seemed to shudder around them.

"Everin, we need to move!" he shouted, but she couldn't hear him over whatever was clawing inside her.

The temple had woken, and Tariel couldn't shake the feeling that they had just walked Everin straight into the heart of its master.

CHAPTER 30

The Hell's Fire Dragon

The atmosphere in the cavernous chamber trembled as Everin's body began to betray her. Tariel's heart hammered in his chest as he watched her writhe on the stone floor, her cries half-human, half-dragon. She thrashed violently, the sickening snap of bones reshaping filling the air. When he reached out instinctively, she shoved him back with a wild strength that wasn't hers. The blow sent him stumbling, nearly knocking him into one of the temple's jagged pillars.

Tariya rushed forward, hand outstretched to help, but Everin's arm lashed out again, her claws raking through the air. The strike didn't touch flesh, but the sheer force hurled Tariya across the chamber, slamming her against the wall.

"Everin, stop!" Tariel shouted, his voice hoarse with desperation. But her glowing eyes were devoid of human emotion and consumed in hell's rage.

Her body twisted and contorted, stretching beyond human limits until the three-headed, Hell's Fire Dragon stood in her place. Black, leathery scales shimmered under the dim light, each one etched with markings: twisting, forked flame-like patterns that seemed to crawl across her body like living brands. No dragon Tariel had ever seen bore such designs. These were the infamous and dreaded markings of hell, which made her the "Feared One." Jagged horns burst from her skull, and wings unfolded with a crack like thunder.

When she roared, it wasn't just a sound; it was a storm that shook the dark walls, raining dust and fragments of stone.

"I command all the dragons now!" Everin's voice, warped into something monstrous, bellowed from three throats at once. "You will bow. You will submit!"

Tariya shifted instantly, silver scales flashing into place as she stood defiant. But compared to the Hell's Fire Dragon, she looked like a hatchling against a mountain.

Her voice was sharp as steel, but her body trembled. "You're not our leader, Everin!" she roared and launched herself upward.

Tariel's breath caught, watching brave, reckless Tariya throw herself at that nightmare. She struck for the rightmost head, claws bared.

One head turned with terrifying speed. Everin snapped her jaws around Tariya's flank and flung her across the cavern. The impact split the stone floor, leaving cracks that spread like lightning. Tariya groaned, blood seeping from her snout, but she pushed herself up, staggering to her claws.

"Everin, please!" she cried, her voice breaking with pain. But the dragon only laughed, a sound so wrong Tariel felt it in his bones.

He clenched his fists, shame burning hotter than fear. He had no dragon form to answer with, no scales to shield him. But he had his sapphire shaft. He swung it into his hands, the weapon elongating with a snap of blue light. His dragon energy surged into it, crackling along the spells carved in its length.

"Everin!" he called, the words spilling in the ancient tongue, words he did not think yet somehow knew. His voice resonated in the chamber, strange and powerful. "Remember who you are. You are not chaos. You are not his puppet. Control your dragon self; do not let the dragon control you."

For a fleeting instant, the middle head hesitated. He swore he saw recognition flicker in those green eyes. But then the left head whipped around, striking him like a hammer. The blow threw him across the stone, his ribs screaming as he slid to the floor.

He coughed blood, forcing himself up, every breath agony. Still, he gripped the shaft. He would not stop. Not while she was lost inside that monster.

Tariya tried again, leaping for the dragon's throat, but Everin's tail lashed out and smashed her into the wall. She crumpled, gasping for air, her dragon form flickering from the pain.

Tariel staggered to his feet, staring up at the creature that had once been his Everin. The thought cut into him like a blade. She was newly transformed, untrained and uncontrolled, yet she was already this powerful. If she had the experience of a seasoned dragon, they would stand no chance at all, he realized grimly.

Then his eyes caught something: a faint glimmer in the chest of Tynan's statue. The Stone of Opalia.

"That's it," he rasped. His pulse quickened. The stone was their only chance. He yelled, "I see the stone. Keep her busy Tariya."

He sprinted, weaving between Everin's snapping heads as Tariya clawed her way upright and hurled herself at the left head, screaming in fury to buy him time. Tariel clambered up the statue, his fingers raw against the rough stone. As he reached the chest, he seized the glowing gem.

The moment his hand closed on it, red lightning surged into him. Agony ripped through his veins, every muscle seizing. His vision flared crimson, and his scream tore the chamber apart. The stone fell from his hand. For one terrible heartbeat, he felt not his own will but Tynan's rage coursing through him.

"No!" Tariya screamed, flying toward him, but the Hell's Fire Dragon lunged. One head struck for her, its jaws gaping.

Tariya dove, human again in a blink, snatching the fallen stone off the ground. She hurled it with all her strength straight into the Hell's Fire dragon's middle mouth.

The effect was instant. Everin's three heads snapped back in unison, a scream of agony blasting from her throats. The stone seared down her gullet, and her entire body convulsed. Green-orange flames poured out, scalding the floor. Her massive form writhed and cracked, the hellish markings on her scales burning red before exploding into ash.

Tariel's heart broke even as he watched. "Everin!" he cried, his voice ragged, but he dared not stop it.

The Hell's Fire Dragon collapsed, splitting apart into a storm of fire and smoke until only Everin's small human body lay trembling on the stone.

Silence fell, broken only by Tariya's rasping breaths as she collapsed at Everin's side.

"She's... she's back," she whispered, tears streaking her bruised face.

But the victory curdled instantly. Tariel's body buckled, still glowing with the cursed red light. He dropped to his knees, then to the floor, twitching as the demonic energy of the statue continued to claw through him. His scream echoed against the temple walls, raw and endless.

The last thing he saw before the darkness took him was Everin, fragile and unconscious, and Tariya's horrified eyes. He realized then that it wasn't over.

The fight had only just begun.

CHAPTER 31

Flames of Betrayal

The candles of the dungeon sputtered under the draft, their flames bending in one direction as though even fire itself recoiled from what had just occurred. The chamber smelled of scorched stone, sulfur, and blood, and the very walls seemed to breathe with the lingering echoes of battle.

Everin stirred, her body weak and drenched in sweat, her limbs heavy as though chains still bound them. She forced herself upright, her hands trembling as she pressed against the icy stone floor, the echo of claws and wings still ringing in her bones.

The first thing she saw was him.

Tariel lay only a few steps away, sprawled on the ground, his chest barely rising, his skin pale and clammy as if the life had been drained from him. Each shallow gasp he made was a blade to her heart. The memory of her own three heads that were snarling, snapping, and spitting fire flashed in her mind, and nausea gripped her. *I did this. I fought them. I almost killed him.*

"Tariel..." Her voice cracked, raw with guilt.

Crawling across the cold floor, she knelt beside him, her shaking hands pressing to his chest as if her touch could call him back. His skin was damp, his pulse faint under her fingers. She brushed her palm against his cheek, her tears stinging as they fell.

Behind her, Tariya sagged against the wall, blood streaking her temple, her body battered and bruised from her transformation and the blows she had taken. Her silver scales had receded, leaving pale skin marked with deep bruises. Her breath came ragged, each inhale sharp, but her eyes, though filled with pain, were focused on Everin and Tariel.

"Is he... alive?" Tariya asked, her voice hoarse, stripped of her usual sharpness, her words more plea than question.

Everin could only shake her head helplessly. "I don't know. I couldn't stop it. When the Hell's Fire Dragon takes me, it's like I'm trapped inside my own body, as if it's not me at all. It commands me. It controls me. I tried, but..." Her voice broke, and she pressed her forehead against Tariel's chest. "I couldn't stop myself from hurting you both."

For once, Tariya didn't argue or mock. She only nodded, her lips tightening, her silence carrying the weight of truth.

The silence was shattered by the echo of heavy boots striking stone. Footsteps, deliberate and unhurried, carried down the passage until two figures burst through the doorway. The sight of them sent Everin's heart into her throat.

Professor Stark swept into the chamber first, her sharp gaze cutting through the chaos. Professor Rudiff followed, his tall frame casting long shadows against the stone walls, his expression unreadable.

"Everin!" Stark's voice cracked with urgency, her eyes widening with relief. "Are you all right?"

Everin managed only a shallow nod, though her eyes never left Tariel. "He... he isn't waking up."

Stark was already at his side, kneeling swiftly, her hands pressing against his pulse, her face grim. "He's alive. But he's weak. We have to move him quickly before..."

Rudiff bent, his shadow falling across them, and placed his hand on Tariel's shoulder. His touch was unnervingly calm, almost gentle. "Come now," he murmured under his breath. "Wake up, boy."

A shudder passed through Tariel's body. His chest hitched, his eyes fluttered, and then he gasped sharply as though surfacing from drowning. His gaze darted wildly until it landed on Everin.

"Tariel!" Everin cried, grasping his arm with both hands. Relief and guilt tangled inside her chest, flooding her voice. "You're alive."

He blinked at her, his voice ragged. "The energy from the statue burned through me. I thought…"

"You're safe now," Stark interrupted, though her words carried the weight of fear beneath their veneer of calm.

For a fleeting moment, Everin thought they had been given a chance to breathe. But then the sound came.

The crunch of boots on stone. Slow, deliberate, and growing louder.

The shadows stretched long against the walls, and then six figures emerged from the passage. They came in formation, men and women dressed in black suits, their faces cold and impassive, their movements fluid like soldiers who had done this countless times before. At their head strode a tall man with slicked-back black hair and a cruel smile that never touched his eyes. His broad shoulders and the heat shimmering around his clenched fists made him a figure impossible to ignore.

"Boss Kael," Everin whispered, her stomach dropping as recognition gripped her. These were the same men who had cornered them in the museum.

Kael's eyes found her instantly, and his smile widened like that of a predator. "At last," he said smoothly, his voice curling through the air like smoke. "We've come for the girl. Hand her over, and the rest of you may live."

Everin rose instinctively, her body trembling but resolute as she placed herself between Tariel and the men. Her heart hammered, but her voice, though wavering, carried defiance. "You'll have to kill me first."

Stark stepped forward, her gaze locked on Kael, her voice sharp and cutting. "Not while I'm here."

Kael chuckled, the sound low and mocking, like embers crackling before a blaze. "Then you've chosen the hard way." He raised his hand, motioning his soldiers forward.

But before they could move, Rudiff's voice cut through the tension.

"Wait," he said, as if it were an order.

The command froze them mid-step. All eyes turned.

Rudiff straightened, and for the first time, Everin saw the truth in his face. The calm professor's mask slid away, replaced by a sly smile that dripped venom. His eyes gleamed cold and cruel, and the sight sent a shiver crawling down her spine.

"You should have known," Rudiff said softly, his voice suddenly alien, filled with an oily satisfaction. "Every lead, every word I shared was to bring you here, Everin. To your master."

Everin's stomach twisted. Her voice shook. "You… you betrayed us?"

"Betrayed?" Rudiff let out a harsh laugh that echoed through the chamber. "No. I was fulfilling my purpose. I was placed at the Academy by the Order of Lord Tynan. We know that only the Lord's reign will free us from the unfair heavenly laws in the mortal realm. Do you truly think it was a coincidence that I appeared when I did? The first step was to remove the Professor of Combat, that tiresome old fool. He stood in our way. Once he was gone, I had my opening. I entered your lives freely, cloaked in authority, and you welcomed me."

Stark's eyes narrowed, her voice like a whip. "So every task, every lesson you guided them was it all deliberate?"

"Of course," Rudiff hissed, his grin widening. "That book in the Restricted Section? I placed it there myself, slipped it into Stark's pile so you'd find it. And I was watching when you uncovered it, whispering about the elixir. And the Moonlight Revels?" He chuckled darkly, his gaze sliding to Everin. "When Phoenix and Zale Nightwind triumphed, it was I who placed the Veilvine's sap vial on the shield. I just wanted to ensure you had all the ingredients for the elixir."

Tariel's fists clenched, fury trembling in his voice. "And Ashmomere… the night we gathered Emberroot? That was you too, wasn't it?"

"Very good, Fenwick." Rudiff's smile turned crueler still. "Yes. Stark patrolled the grounds that night, but I was the one who lowered the barriers around the tent. I gave you the opportunity to succeed, to collect the Emberroot, all the while pretending to stand as your protector. Every trial, every struggle was carefully placed stones on the path toward awakening Everin's true nature."

Tariel's eyes blazed, his voice sharp with disbelief. "And New

York? The day we arrived?"

Rudiff's tone darkened, his words laced with satisfaction. "Ah, yes. That was to be the moment. The Order's plan was to bring Everin straight to the Temple of Lord Tynan. She was meant to awaken then and there, before her father could meddle. His sudden presence forced us to delay, to adjust. But even that obstacle could not halt destiny."

Everin's voice was a broken whisper. "You used us… all of us."

"Used?" Rudiff sneered, his eyes gleaming with fanatic light. "No, girl. I guided you. Without me, you would still be a frightened child fumbling in the dark. It was I who shaped you into the Hell's Fire Dragon. The 'Feared One.' And now the whole dragon world will fear you."

Professor Stark's jaw tightened, her voice sharp. "And the Stone of Opalia? Was that part of your plan too?"

Rudiff waved a dismissive hand. "When Fenwick got the Book of Dracos and mentioned the Stone of Opalia, the Order saw this as an opportunity to get Everin out of the Academy. The stone is irrelevant. It's just a trinket. The true purpose has always been you, Everin. The Order never cared about relics or councils or schools. The only goal was to bring you here, to the

Temple of Lord Tynan, so your powers could awaken in the shadow of your master, before his return. You are his heir. His chosen. And soon, you will embrace it fully."

Tariya's fists clenched as she accused him, "You betrayed us all."

His smirk deepened. "Not betrayed. I fulfilled my job. I am one of them. We are the Order of Lord Tynan. We've waited centuries for this moment—for Everin. For the Hell's Fire Dragon. The true heir of chaos." His eyes glimmered as they locked on her. "You will rule, Everin. The Order will kneel at your feet, and so will the world. This is your destiny."

Her fists clenched so tight her nails bit into her skin. "I am no one's leader and certainly no demon lord's servant," she spat, glaring at the looming statue of Tynan. "And I never will be."

Rudiff's smile grew sharper, his voice coaxing, pouring like honeyed poison. "You already feel it, don't you? The power. The hunger. You cannot deny it. You are his chosen. Stop fighting what you are, and the world will burn at your command."

Kael sneered, his hands blazing with heat. "Enough talk. Take her."

The soldiers surged forward.

And Everin broke.

The Stone of Opalia, buried in the depths of her body now, pulsed with a terrible heat, its light searing her skin. Her chest convulsed as darkness swept over her, her body trembling violently. Pain shot through every vein, every bone, as the dragon roared awake inside her. Her scream echoed, twisting into a roar that shook the foundations.

Her skin blackened, her body stretched, wings tearing forth. Three heads unfurled, each one shrieking with rage, fire spilling from their jaws.

The Hell's Fire Dragon rose, monstrous and unstoppable. "I didn't know she had already transformed!" Kael shouted, shock cracking through his composure.

Rudiff's eyes gleamed with triumph. "Wasn't that the point of bringing her here?"

Chaos erupted.

Everin's three heads snapped at the soldiers, flames engulfing two instantly, their screams silenced by fire. Her tail lashed, smashing stone and bodies alike. One head spat a torrent of green-orange hellfire, forcing Kael to dive aside, his coat aflame as he cursed.

Stark moved with deadly precision, conjuring spheres of crackling blue energy and hurling them into Rudiff's path as he tried to retreat. One struck him, sending him sprawling, but before he could recover, a torrent of Everin's flame seared his robes, leaving him writhing and screaming.

Tariya, though battered and bloody, transformed again, her small white dragon form leaping at two soldiers. She tore into them with claws and teeth, her courage outweighing her size.

Kael's sneer twisted into something darker. His body convulsed, bones cracking and stretching as scales erupted across his skin. His form grew larger and larger until the man was gone, replaced by a massive dragon of burnished brown and deep amber, his wings fanning out wide enough to rattle the dungeon walls. His eyes glowed molten orange, and when he opened his jaws, fire poured out in a torrent of pure rage.

"Face me then, beast," Kael's voice thundered, distorted by his dragon form.

Everin reared back, her three heads rising high, green flames pouring from her throats as her eyes flashed with emerald fire. Her roar split the air, shaking dust and stones loose from the ceiling. She lunged, her left head snapping at Kael's throat, her middle one spewing a torrent of searing orange-green flame.

Kael countered with brute force. His claws raked against her scales, sparks flying as metal scraped against stone. He twisted, his wings slamming her sideways into the cavern wall, and his flame blasted against her flank, scorching black across her glowing scales. Everin howled in fury, her right head lashing at him and sinking teeth into the thick scales at his shoulder. Blood, dark and smoking, sprayed across the floor as Kael roared, thrashing to free himself.

The chamber was an inferno. Stone cracked, shallow stream water surged, and the statue of Tynan loomed through the haze, its carved grin lit by firelight as if he savored the destruction.

Tariya launched into the air, her small silver dragon form a dart of light against the chaos. She snapped her claws into the chest of a soldier who had transformed mid-fight, an obsidian-scaled girl with wings like a bat and a hiss sharp as knives. The two clashed, spinning through the air, fire and sparks exploding as claws and tails collided. Tariya fought with desperate precision, her smaller size forcing her to be faster, more cunning.

Everin's three heads turned in fury, one snapping Kael's wing, another claw raking down his flank. Kael staggered but retaliated with a violent strike of his tail. The blow was so forceful it sent her crashing across the chamber floor, stone cracking beneath her massive body. Her roar filled the dungeon, but for the first time, pain flickered in her eyes.

"Everin!" Tariel's voice rang out.

He staggered forward, still weak from the statue's blast, but his sapphire shaft glowed fiercely in his grip. He poured what dragon energy he could summon into it, the gem at its head flaring with an azure light. As Kael reared back, jaws opening to scorch Everin's fallen body, Tariel thrust the shaft forward.

A torrent of blue fire shot from the weapon, striking Kael's snout with explosive force. The adult dragon roared in pain, recoiling, smoke and blood pouring from his nostrils.

Everin seized the moment. Her three heads reared, eyes blazing with terrible clarity. "You will not break me!" she thundered, her middle throat releasing a blast of searing orange-green hellfire straight into Kael's chest. His scales blackened under the torrent, his wings faltered, and with a pained bellow, he stumbled back, crashing against the base of Tynan's statue.

Across the chamber, Tariya slammed her enemy against the

wall, her silver claws pressing into the girl's dark scales until she screeched and yielded, slumping to the floor. Tariya, bloodied but relentless, turned back to watch Everin tower above Kael.

Kael roared one last time, but his strength faltered. His body shuddered, his dragon form shrinking back into his battered human shape. Smoke poured from his wounds, his breath ragged, his face twisted in fury as he staggered to one knee.

"Retreat!" Rudiff barked suddenly, his mask of calm gone, his voice sharp with panic. He motioned to the remaining men, his own robe smoldering where Everin's flame had caught him. "Fall back! Now!"

The black-suited soldiers obeyed instantly, dragging their injured with them, their footsteps echoing in chaotic retreat. Kael, cursing under his breath, staggered to his feet, his glare fixed on Everin's towering form. Then, with one last snarl, he vanished into the shadows with Rudiff and the rest of his men.

The dungeon fell silent except for the crackle of lingering flames as dust and smoke hung thick in the air.

Everin stood in the heart of it all, her three heads still blazing, fire dripping from her jaws. But she did not kill. Not one body lay dead, only scorched and broken, left behind as reminders.

Slowly, her flames dimmed, her breathing steadied. Her glowing eyes turned toward Tariel.

He stood there, leaning heavily on the sapphire shaft, his chest heaving, sweat streaking his brow, but his eyes, those clear, determined eyes, were locked on hers.

"You're still you," he whispered again, hoarse but certain.

Everin's three heads bowed slightly, and her resonant voice rolled through the cavern. "And I will never let anyone control me again."

As Everin stood tall, the weight of her newfound power settling within her, she knew the road ahead would be long and uncertain. But for the first time, she felt ready to face whatever came next.

CHAPTER 32

The Forces of Fate

A week had passed since the harrowing events that unfolded deep within the dungeon beneath St. Paul's Chapel. Everin had spent most of that week in the quiet isolation of her thoughts, trying to come to terms with the terrifying powers that had awakened within her. The dragon's ferocity still lingered in her veins, but it was now tempered by the knowledge that she had control, at least, for now. Her dragon form, the Hell's Fire Dragon, had the power to bring about chaos, but the Stone of Opalia, it seemed, kept that darkness at bay. For how long, though, she couldn't be sure.

Today, however, would mark a turning point.

Everin stood in front of the Chief Professor's office at Drakon Academy, her feet unwilling to move further as she stared at the intricately carved wooden door. She could hear the muffled voices coming from within: Professor Stark's calm tones, and the deeper, more deliberate voice of Chief Professor Decimus Fenwick, the Headmaster.

Taking a deep breath, she knocked lightly and then pushed the door open. The faint scent of wood and parchment greeted her as she stepped into the spacious office. Tall shelves lined the walls, filled with ancient books and scrolls, and a massive wooden desk sat in the center of the room, cluttered with papers and open books. Fenwick, tall and rugged, was seated behind it, flipping through a thick book. His sharp gaze met hers as she entered, and he offered her a reassuring smile, though it didn't reach his tired eyes.

"Everin," he greeted her, his voice warm yet heavy. "Come in. Have a seat."

Professor Stark, standing nearby, offered a nod of encouragement. Her usual stern expression softened when her eyes met Everin's, and she gestured to the empty chair opposite Fenwick. Everin took a seat, feeling the weight of the room settle over her. This wasn't just another meeting; this was the moment when everything about her future at the Academy would be decided.

"We've received word from the Council of the Dragons of the West," Fenwick began, closing the book he had been writing in. "They have decided to let you continue your studies here at Drakon Academy."

Everin's heart skipped a beat. She had been dreading this conversation, uncertain of whether the Council would allow her to stay or whether she would be exiled for the danger she represented. But to her surprise, Fenwick's words were a lifeline.

"You mean… I'm not being sent away?" she asked, her voice betraying the relief she felt.

Fenwick nodded slowly. "No, not for now. The Council recognizes that you are still in control of your powers. And as for the Hell's Fire Dragon, the Stone of Opalia seems to be holding that back, for now. The Book of Dracos suggests that the stone can be used to maintain control over the dragon, so we are safe, for the moment."

Everin felt a weight lift off her chest, but there was still a nagging worry in the back of her mind. "And the demon, the one who is supposed to rise if I lose control?"

Stark's gaze hardened. "Tynan, the Demon of Darkness and Chaos. Apparently, the Council is concerned, but for now, they've left the matter in your hands. The truth is, Everin, the demon's awakening depends on you. And while the Stone of Opalia can suppress his influence, the question remains: how long can you keep control before the demon finds a way in?"

Everin's stomach turned at the thought. She had no desire to become the vessel for Tynan's darkness, but she had no idea how long she could hold him back. What if she lost control one day? What if the darkness took over completely?

Fenwick, sensing her unease, leaned forward, his voice gentle but firm. "We have faith in you. The Council may be keeping its distance for now, but they've allowed you to stay. That's a step forward."

Everin nodded, swallowing hard. "I won't let the demon possess me," she said, more to herself than anyone else. "Not ever."

Professor Stark gave her a small, approving smile, and for a moment, the weight of the conversation lifted. But before she could ask anything else, a question lingered in her mind, one she had been too afraid to ask until now.

"What about the people who wanted to take me?" Everin asked. "Rudiff's group, those men who were after me?"

Fenwick's face darkened at the mention of the traitorous professor. "They were likely part of a larger organization. They wanted to capture you because you are the key to awakening Tynan. You are the vessel, the one who can either bring him into the world or keep him locked away."

Everin's mind raced as she tried to process the meaning of Fenwick's words. Her existence was more than just an anomaly; she was the key to a catastrophic chain of events, and there were people willing to do anything to see that it unfolded. The thought was terrifying.

"But I won't let that happen," she said resolutely, her voice firm despite the tremor in her hands. "I'll make sure the demon never gets his chance."

Professor Stark nodded approvingly. "That's the spirit, Everin. The road ahead won't be easy, but we'll help you every step of the way."

With that, the conversation seemed to wind down. But Everin's mind kept spinning, the weight of the world on her shoulders. She wasn't just a student at Drakon Academy anymore; she was a weapon, a potential savior, or a ticking time bomb, depending on which way the winds of fate blew.

At midday, the Academy's grand assembly hall was filled with hushed whispers that rose and fell like waves breaking against stone. Sunlight spilled through tall arched windows, painting the room in shades of gold and silver, yet the warmth of the light couldn't melt the icy weight pressing down on Everin's chest.

As she entered with Tariel, Phoenix, Jackson, and Tariya, heads turned. Dozens of students stared, some curious, others wary, while a few were openly hostile. The air thickened with judgment. Everin's steps faltered for a heartbeat, but Tariel's steady hand brushed lightly against hers, unseen by most. The contact grounded her. She lifted her chin and kept walking.

They found a place near the center, all five sitting close together as though daring anyone to pry them apart. Phoenix crossed her arms and glared at a group of older students who were whispering too loudly. Jackson leaned forward, his voice low but sharp. "If they've got something to say, they can say it to us."

Tariya smirked, tossing her braid over her shoulder. "Let them talk. They weren't the ones fighting a group of dragons in the streets of New York City." Her tone was dry, but the loyalty in her words was unmistakable.

Everin blinked hard, surprised by the sudden swell of gratitude. For days, she had felt like a deadly animal that was feared, mistrusted, whispered about, but here, surrounded by her friends, she realized she wasn't alone. They were choosing to stand with her. Even Tariel, quiet as ever, was a presence so strong she could feel his calm radiating beside her. His arm brushed hers again, just enough to tell her: I'm here.

Still, the words of others stung.

Zale, lounging arrogantly near the front, made his feelings clear, his voice carrying deliberately. "My father is furious that the Council still allows her to stay. He says she should be locked in the Abyssagon, the dragon dungeons, far away from the rest of us."

Some students gasped at the mention of Abyssagon, because it was a cursed place for the notoriously dangerous and convicted dragons.

Everin's stomach twisted.

Rhodes, never one to be subtle, muttered loudly, "She's a monster. One mistake, and she'll burn us all."

A ripple of laughter followed.

Everin's throat tightened, but before she could respond, Phoenix leaned back in her chair, her voice sharp as a whip. "Funny, Rhodes. Maybe you should fight a dozen dragon shapeshifters and see if you can make it back to the Academy or not."

Jackson chuckled darkly at her side, adding, "Careful, Phoenix, you'll bruise his ego."

Tariya simply rolled her eyes and muttered, "Pathetic," loud enough for half the hall to hear.

The sting of their words eased, replaced with the glow of loyalty. Everin glanced at Tariel. He wasn't speaking, but his eyes met hers, steady and unwavering. She swallowed hard. For a moment, the weight of fear pressing down on her shoulders lessened.

Then Selene, one of the fashionable final years, laughed cruelly. "Wouldn't it be cool to be the Feared One? You would be trending on Drakon Deeds, no matter what you do."

Everin pursed her lips because Drakon Deeds was the Academy's social media app, where she had been trending lately.

That was the breaking point.

Everin stood, her hands trembling but her voice steady.
The hall fell into silence, all eyes locking onto her. Her heart pounded, but she refused to shrink back.

"I didn't choose this," she said, her voice ringing through the chamber. "I didn't ask for it. But I'm not a monster. I'm not your enemy. I will fight for control, and I will prove to you that I am not the thing you should fear."

Silence stretched long and heavy. Her pulse thudded in her ears. Then, softly and slowly, Tariya began to clap. "Well said," she declared, rising to her feet. Phoenix followed, her eyes fierce. Jackson stood too, his hands striking together with firm conviction.

And finally, Tariel rose, his gaze never leaving Everin's. His clap was softer, slower, but the pride in his eyes was unmistakable. She felt her breath catch.

The applause spread across the hall in uneven waves. Not everyone joined, but enough did. Enough to remind her she wasn't entirely alone.

Later, the hall fell silent as Chief Mariah Mac Naught stepped onto the stage, her silver hair gleaming like spun moonlight. She carried herself with the authority of centuries, yet her smile softened as her gaze fell on Tariya.

"With courage beyond her years, Tariya Gratton stood against odds that would have broken many," Mariah announced. "Her loyalty to her friends, her willingness to fight despite the danger, speaks to the very heart of what it means to be a dragon."

She held out a polished crystal crest, which was the Courageous Award. Tariya's eyes widened, her lips parting in disbelief as she stepped forward to accept it. The hall erupted into applause, louder this time, genuine and proud.

Everin clapped too, warmth filling her chest as she watched Tariya's grin break across her bruised face. Yet beneath the pride, a pang cut through her. She leaned close to Tariel and whispered, "No one gives awards to a Feared One."

Tariel's lips curved into a wry, dry smile. "No one cares about your bravery until you can transform properly, Everin. Believe me, I know."

His words struck her with quiet force. For the first time, she truly understood the ache he carried, the shame of being a late bloomer, and the sting of judgment. She whispered back, her voice almost breaking, "Yes, we both know."

Tariel's gaze softened, and for a fleeting moment, she felt seen. Not as the Feared One. Not as the Hell's Fire Dragon. Just as Everin.

Later that afternoon, the Academy grounds had settled into a rare stillness, though Everin's mind hadn't slowed once. She sat by the water fountain, the cool spray misting against her skin, her heart heavy with the weight of the assembly and all the eyes that had burned into her. Phoenix plopped down beside her with a sigh, tossing her golden hair back, while Tariya leaned against the stone edge, sipping from a flask of water she had carried everywhere since their last mission.

"You both realize," Phoenix said with a smirk, "that if we were normal, we'd be gossiping about crushes and hairstyles right now instead of demons and fire dragons."

"Normal's boring," Tariya muttered, her tone flat but her lips twitching into the smallest of grins.

Everin let out a laugh, faint but real. "I don't know... boring sounds kind of amazing right now."

Phoenix reached over and nudged her shoulder. "Well, until then, you're stuck with us. And we're not going anywhere. So, deal with it."

The three of them sat there for a moment, their laughter blending with the bubbling of the fountain. For a heartbeat, Everin almost believed she was just another student, sharing an afternoon with her friends.

But then, Phoenix stood and announced that they should all

go for "some fashion therapy" to get rid of the day's stress.

"Oh no," moaned Tariya as she slumped further in her seat.

"It won't work today. You are coming with me. Now." Phoenix pulled Tariya to her feet.

Before Phoenix targeted her, Everin quickly came up with an excuse.

"Go ahead," she said lightly. "I'll catch up. I just want to call my dad first."

"Don't take too long," Tariya warned, narrowing her eyes as though she didn't fully believe her. "If you start sulking out here all night, I'll drag you back myself."

Phoenix rolled her eyes. "Come on, Tariya. She's fine. She's got that dreamy boyfriend of hers to brood over." She winked at Everin, earning a blush, before the two disappeared toward the dormitories.

The moment they were gone, silence pressed in. Everin pulled out her phone and called her father, Marcus Haydon. His face lit the screen, familiar and grounding.

"Hey, Dad," she said softly, her voice barely above the sound of the fountain. "I'm doing okay. A little more in control, I think."

"Good," Marcus replied, his voice steady and warm. "Just remember, don't lose sight of who you are, no matter what happens. You're my daughter before you're anything else."

The knot in her chest loosened slightly. "Thanks, Dad. I needed that."

When the call ended, she set her phone down and stared at the rippling water. For a fleeting moment, she felt peace.

Then it came.

A voice. Cold. Sharp. Not her father's, not her own thoughts.

"Get up."

Everin froze, her breath catching. The command sliced through her mind like a blade. Her body trembled as the words repeated, relentless.

"Come to me, now."

Her legs moved before she could think. She rose, each step heavier than the last yet impossible to resist. Her pulse hammered in her ears, her throat dry as if she were suffocating.

"Tariya…" she tried to whisper, but the name fell uselessly into the empty courtyard. They were gone. She was alone.

She held onto her chest, hoping to feel the Stone of Opalia, anxiously in case it could stop that commanding voice in her head.

But her body responded before her brain could defy the order.

Her feet carried her toward the forest, faster, and faster. Until she was running, branches clawing at her arms, and shadows swallowing the last late afternoon light. The compulsion grew stronger with each step, pulling her deeper into the trees.

The forest opened into a clearing. Evening spilled across the ground, golden against the black earth. And there, waiting, was a figure cloaked in darkness. Tall, imposing, his face hidden in shadow.

Everin's breath left her lungs in a rush, her body trembling as the voice in her head fell silent, replaced by the sound of his real one.

"You've come."

She sank to the ground on her knees. Her lips parted, the word slipping out before she could stop it, soft and terrified.

"Master."

About the Author

La Kayshal is an Australian writer of romance, YA, and children's fantasy novels. She lives with her husband, daughter, and a playful Malshi puppy in the coastal plains of the Sunny State.

Her debut novel, **The Lost Crown**, is an adventure romance set in the exotic landscapes of India. She also created the much-loved **Sylph Series**, a whimsical children's collection that introduces readers to the amazing world of Sylphs, with each book carrying a gentle moral lesson.

A lifelong fan of wizards, magic, dragons, swords, and elementals, she poured all these passions into her YA fantasy **Ariston Baker in the Weird Picture Book**, a fast-paced journey filled with realms, riddles, action, and adventure.

Her latest project is the Hell's Fire Dragon series. Book 1, **The Flames of Darkness**, is a YA Romantasy full of dragons, and Book 2 is set to be released soon.